Clairvoyance

Clairvoyance

KRISTIANA
KAHAKAUWILA

HARPER

An Imprint of HarperCollinsPublishers

Library of Congress Control Number: 2023943341
ISBN 978-0-06-304535-4

Typography by Corina Lupp
24 25 26 27 28 LBC 5 4 3 2 1

First Edition

for my grandmothers
Clara and Larita
&
for Aila
and her kūpuna

He keiki mea kupuna.

One

"GIVE ME BACK MY 'UKULELE."

The voice of Pua, the new girl, rises above the usual bus chatter.

"What, you no trust us?" Brandon teases.

"Put it back in the case!" Pua pleads. Her eyes grow wider as she turns from Brandon to Denny to my ex–best friend, Leo.

It's no use, I want to tell her. The key to keeping anything safe on our school bus is to hold it in your lap. I probably should have given Pua that advice when she tucked her 'ukulele case under the seat. But now it's too late. Brandon strums roughly on the uke's strings, making them vibrate harshly. Then he passes the instrument to Denny, who tries to balance it on three fingers.

"It's delicate!" Pua protests.

That just makes Denny laugh and try to balance the uke on one finger. "Look, I'm LeBron!"

"You're Le-*Gone*, dude," Brandon shoots back. "You have as many ups as Mouse over there." I barely have to sink down in my seat to disappear.

It's true that Denny is the second-shortest kid in our class, but he's really athletic. I've seen him on a basketball court, and he'll run circles around anyone, even someone as tall as Brandon. But that doesn't mean Denny can balance an uke on his finger forever. The second before the 'ukulele falls, Leo scoops it up. "Hey, I had it!" Denny shouts.

Leo doesn't answer. Instead, he fiddles with the pegs.

"What are you doing?" Pua asks, panicked.

Leo strums a couple of chords and smiles. The uke is back in tune.

"Are you going to play for us?" Michelle leans into the aisle and smiles sweetly up at him.

Leo runs his fingers along his fade. He keeps his hair long on top, a volcano of tight curls, the same style his dad used to wear. "What you like hear?"

"Something good." Michelle tosses her long hair from one shoulder to the other. The golden highlights catch the afternoon sun. Only Michelle could perfect a move like that. Both she and her best friend, Crystal, have danced hula since they were two, but it's Michelle who moves through the world as if it's her stage and the rest of us are merely her audience.

"Can't you tell him to stop?" Pua begs.

Michelle levels her with an eye roll. "If Leo like play, he like play." She's the queen of the code switch, moving between English and pidgin with ease. It's not just Hawaiian Creole she speaks either; she's already taking the advanced ʻōlelo Hawaiʻi class at school. "You mainland types are so uptight. Isn't that right, Baby Mouse?" She makes a point of looking my way.

I slide even lower in my seat. I *hate* that nickname. But Michelle seems determined to make it stick.

Pua turns to me, desperate. "Can't you . . . ?"

I shake my head. I have no power in this situation.

The one saving grace for Pua is that Leo can play the ʻukulele. Not just play, jam. When we were still friends, he used to practice in my tūtū's garden while I sketched the finches and sparrows that came to visit our taro patches. He'd have Tūtū dancing in no time.

Now Leo strums a chorus before crooning: "Country road, take me home, to the place I belong."

"Waialua," Denny calls out.

"Haleʻiwa," Leo sings back. "Take me home, Kumu Maka, take me home." Leo hits the last chord with a flourish and the guys laugh and clap. Kumu Maka, our bus driver, glances up into the rearview mirror and smiles.

"You never said you was one regular Iz." Brandon slaps Leo on the back. Iz was a Hawaiian singer who died years ago, but everyone—our grandparents, our parents, us—still loves him. Tūtū used to say Leo could have a voice like Iz's if he practiced, but Leo always said he rather play for fun.

"I like for goof around," Leo says now. He hands the uke back to Pua, all casual. He doesn't even look at her. Yet he's made sure she got her instrument back unharmed.

Pua doesn't know how lucky she is. Our school bus takes all the North Shore stops, starting in Waipiʻo and curving around the top of Oʻahu, then down the east side of the island. An hour or more of that and her instrument definitely would have been damaged.

When the ʻukulele is safely zipped into its case again, Pua moves up three rows to the next empty seat. The one next to me. "Boys!" she exclaims. She sits with the case in her lap, hugging the neck of it to her chest. Pua's skin is fairer than mine, and her straight black hair lies flat, unlike my curly flyaways. But now that we're seated next to each

4

other I see that we're close in height and are wearing the same rainbow Crocs. "I'm Pua. You're Clara, right?"

"Right." I leave it at that. Even if we have a couple of similarities, there's no need to encourage conversation. I'm sure she'll learn soon enough that being friends with me will only drag her down.

I pull my sketchbook out of my backpack. One day, when I convince my dad to stay in Arizona and move me out there, too, I won't bring anyone down anymore. I won't be a baby mouse, scurrying around the edges of school. I'll be someone who soars, out of reach. Like the white-tailed kite I'm drawing.

Kites are cool birds because they can hover over one spot by flying into oncoming wind. This is called kiting. When I was visiting Dad in Phoenix this summer, we saw a bunch of white-tailed kites while we were out hiking. Later, when my friendship with Leo fell apart, Dad told me I had to keep flying into the wind. Stay strong in the face of a storm. All that.

Mom has a different set of flying metaphors. She tells me there comes a time to spread your wings. That, when I'm old enough, I can fly away to a new place, a new life. A new me.

I like Mom's metaphor better.

I've been telling Dad this for two and a half months now, since the beginning of the school year in August. But Dad says he's hesitant to "uproot" me. Back when he and Mom were still together, we moved a bunch: Alabama, Kansas, Texas. From one base to another, following Mom's orders. For Mom, each new post was exciting. For Dad, none of them were home. So when he and Mom split, he took me back to O'ahu, and we moved in with Tūtū.

For a while, everything was perfect. Dad reconnected with old friends. We saw extended family. And the best part was that Dad's besties, Auntie Nina and Uncle Will, were Leo's parents. So Leo became my bestie. For three years—from third through fifth grade—Leo and I were inseparable.

Then all that changed.

Then Leo changed.

Two

THE BUS PULLS OFF THE main road in Wahiawā to drop off Crystal before winding its way to Waialua. That's where Michelle and Brandon say goodbye to Leo and Denny. Finally, we're headed for Haleʻiwa, where Leo lives.

I live another ten minutes past that, on the hillside above a popular snorkel spot called Pūpūkea. Tūtū raised Dad there, and now she is raising me there.

"What are you doing?" Pua asks. She's leaned so far over me that her hair tickles my chin. I press myself against the window.

"Nothing. Just drawing."

"What are you drawing?"

I try to silence her with a stare, like Michelle does to just about everyone, but Pua merely smiles back and I end up giving in. "A white-tailed kite," I say.

"A what?"

"A kite. A type of bird."

I bend over my drawing again, using my arm to block Pua's view. Maybe she'll get the hint and stop asking questions. Instead, she peers under my elbow.

"It looks like a football player wearing shoulder pads," she says with a giggle.

I snap closed my sketchbook. Those are shoulder patches, not pads. I turn toward the window, hoping she'll realize I'm not interested in talking about my art. Or anything else, for that matter.

The bus rumbles down Kamehameha Highway before sighing to a stop near the harbor. Leo, Denny, and a few other kids say goodbye to Kumu Maka before getting off the bus. Outside my window, Leo pauses on the sidewalk to zip up his backpack. Then he does something he hasn't done for months. He gazes up at me and waves. I'm so startled to be caught watching him that I put my sketchbook in front of my face.

Immediately, I regret this move. Did I think the sketchbook would make me invisible?

Pua takes this as her cue to wiggle her fingers at Leo. Figures! *Thank you*, she mouths through the glass.

The bus starts up again and bumps over the little bridge before breezing past the Surf N Sea shop. "You can put down your sketchbook," Pua says. "Leo's gone."

"I know that." I rest the book back on my lap. "I was, um, studying my shading."

"He was trying to get your attention, you know. Why did you hide from him?"

"I wasn't hiding!" I think of all the times this year that I've eaten lunch alone in a stall in the girls' bathroom. Or behind the cafeteria, where the delivery trucks park. I wouldn't call it hiding, exactly. I like to think of it as having space to myself.

"What were you doing, then?"

"Avoiding him."

"Leo was the one who got my 'ukulele back. He doesn't seem like someone who needs avoiding."

"You're new here, so you have no idea."

"Then fill me in. Because from where I'm sitting, Leo seems like the only person on this whole bus worth being friends with."

"I'm worth being friends—" I catch myself. Pua is grinning, and I know she's baiting me into talking. "Leo used to be worth being friends with, too. But now . . ."

Pua spins 180 degrees and crosses her legs, wedging

9

herself against the seat in front of us so she's facing me. "I'm all ears. We've got a long ride ahead still."

I can't avoid Pua when she's sitting like that, and maybe I don't want to. Maybe I want to tell her about what kind of friends Leo and I used to be. The true kind. Through my mom's third deployment and his dad's cancer. Through his dad's passing and my dad's decision to move to Arizona for work. It felt like Leo and I weathered everything together, and I was sure we would always be there for each other.

Then sixth grade started.

I take a deep breath. For Pua, I start the story in the recent past. "Over the summer, I went to visit my dad in Arizona. He's got a job there right now and a girlfriend, and he arranged all these road trips for us. Anyway, I was gone all summer, so Leo started hanging out with Brandon and Denny. When I got back,Leo was too busy with them to catch up with me. But on the first day of school, he waved me over to eat with him and his new friends, so I figured we were good."

I can still picture it. The cafeteria. Everyone in their first-day-of-school clothes. The buzz of questions—*What did you do this summer? OMG, your mom let you dye your hair! Where did you get that backpack?*—and Leo, waving. I felt so cool weaving through the tables to reach him and the others.

"It wasn't just Brandon and Denny. Michelle and Crystal were there, too. At first it was fine. Michelle was talking about the volunteering she had done over the summer and Brandon was talking about the beach, and then Denny asked what I had done. So I pulled out my sketchbook to show them. I'd drawn the huge Ferris wheel in Vegas I rode with my dad. And these cowboy boots that his girlfriend, Steph, bought. I even showed everyone a sketch of a saguaro cactus, which Denny said looked like a boy's— well, you know. But we all laughed. Because only Denny would say something like that out loud. Then I turned to this drawing of Mickey Mouse from when I visited Disneyland, and Michelle burst out, 'If you love the mainland so much, go back there already!'"

Pua gasps. "She said that?"

Finally! I think. *Someone who gets it.* Not even Tūtū reacted like this when I told her.

"What did you say back?" Pua asks.

"I didn't say anything. I looked at Leo. I figured he'd have my back. But then he said, 'You know, she's kind of right, Clara.'" The table went quiet. My face got all hot and I wanted to get away or hide or both. "I stood up to leave, and Leo reached for his milk carton. And the next thing I know there's milk all over my sketchbook. My whole summer of drawings. Everything I had done to capture my trip and my time with my dad. Soaked."

"But it was an accident, right? Leo doesn't seem the type to do that on purpose." Pua has her hands folded and pressed against her chest, like she's praying Leo isn't the bad guy in the story.

"At first, I thought it was an accident, too. But then Michelle goes, 'Wow, Leo, way to show Clara what you really think.'"

"Whoa," Pua says. "That is low."

I squeeze my eyes shut. "And it gets worse."

"How?" Pua is breathless.

"Denny said, 'Oh, look, it's Milky Mouse,' and everyone started laughing. And then"—ugh, I hate to admit to this, but Pua needs to know if she's going to understand why Leo and I don't talk—"I started crying."

"In front of everyone?"

I nod. "And Brandon said really loudly, for everyone to hear, 'Don't be such a baby mouse.' And by the end of the day, our whole grade was calling me Baby Mouse."

"Oh nooooo," Pua groans. "Didn't Leo tell them to stop?"

"He didn't say anything. Not then and not since."

I don't tell Pua every detail. Like how, when I ran out of the cafeteria in tears, Leo didn't come after me. And when I stopped eating lunch with the other sixth graders, he didn't come looking for me then either. And that while he texted once to ask what was wrong, when I didn't text back, he stopped doing even that. Michelle had been right. He had shown me what he really thought of our friendship. So I stopped being friends with him. And everyone else, for that matter.

"If that had happened to me in Seattle, I would have lost it."

"I told Tūtū I never wanted to go back to school, but she told me to wait it out. People would forget about baby mouse. Which, I guess, most of them did."

"Not Michelle, apparently."

"Or Brandon. But it doesn't matter. I'm going to get a fresh start soon enough. I'm going to move to Arizona to be with my dad."

"Fresh starts aren't always easy either, you know." Pua wraps her arms around her ʻukulele case.

"Not always, I guess." I look at Pua with pity. I remember being the new kid, too. In Kansas and Texas. It was hard. When I came here and Leo walked into third grade beside me, I thought the days of being the new kid were over. But then I learned there's something worse than being new. There's being betrayed by your best friend.

As the school bus wheezes into the Foodland parking lot, I spot a dark fleck high in the sky. A bird, I wonder? Or a photographer's drone? Whatever it is, it's hovering above the reef break.

I follow Pua off the bus. "You want a ride home?" she asks. "My mom doesn't mind."

"It's a short walk for me," I lie. The walk is nearly two miles. Uphill.

"Well, maybe you could come over this weekend, then? We can hang out more."

Hang out more? Did Pua already forget the story I told her? Hanging out with me is not going to make her a bunch of new friends. "I kind of fly solo."

"Good bird pun." She laughs. "We're going to get along great."

I study her for a moment. She doesn't know anyone else yet, so she still thinks my puns are funny and my sketchbook is cool. But what happens when she meets more people? Will they want her to leave me out? And will she listen? "I don't think I can—" I start to say. Just then a shadow passes over us, blocking out the sun. Pua and I look up into the sky at the same time.

"Whoa, is that the bird you were drawing on the bus?"

"White-tailed kites don't live in Hawai'i," I answer automatically. But I understand why Pua said what she did. What's above us is definitely a bird, and a large one at that. Pua hasn't noticed the coloring, though. White-tailed kites are mostly white with black shoulders; this bird is a deep black with a tuft of white on its chest. Both birds know how to kite, however. This one floats directly above us.

I'm still staring upward when Pua says, "Are you sure you can't come over?" Her voice is heavy with disappointment.

The bird tilts, as if to catch a different current of air, and then soars toward the mountains. It's a thrilling sight. It makes my heart lift a little. And it makes me want to lift up Pua, too. I turn my attention back to her. "It's more like a maybe," I decide. "I have to ask my tūtū. But, um, remember that I'm leaving soon."

Pua rewards me with a huge smile. "I'm happy being friends until you go."

Three

I WISH I WAS A bird that could fly up the hill to Tūtū's house. Instead, I'm stuck on two feet. The humid air makes my skin sticky, and by the time I reach home, I am dripping with sweat. I head straight for our backyard, to the patio Dad built, with its shaded pergola and picnic table. Here the breeze rolls up from the ocean, and the 'auwai—the ditch that siphons water from the mountain stream—keeps the land lush and cool. I take a seat on a picnic bench and grab the pair of binoculars we keep outside for bird-watching. No cute songbirds today, but I spot Tūtū right away.

Tūtū is bent over the 'auwai clearing leaves and branches so the water can flow easily among our taro patches. When she sees me, she waves. Beyond her, a neighbor's rooftop glints with solar panels, and somewhere to my left, hidden behind trees and rooflines, is Puʻokinau-o-mahuka heiau. Tūtū says that heiau was once the largest religious site on the island of Oʻahu. Farther beneath us, the ocean is so blue that I can't tell where the water ends and the sky begins. But, in my opinion, none of that compares to what's right in front of me.

There's our garden where we grow lettuce, tomatoes, cucumbers, and other vegetables. Our fruit trees that give us mountain apples, papayas, and mangoes. Our ʻōhiʻa lehua, with bright red flowers exploding like fireworks amid the dusty green leaves. And finally, on the gentlest decline of the property, is our loʻi—the rectangular paddies where we grow our taro.

As Tūtū hikes up the hillside, she scrolls through her phone. I bet she's looking for one of her favorite streaming stations, something to match her mood. She's wearing a faded T-shirt from the '70s with the band name Commodores printed across it in bright blues and pinks. As she reaches the lānai, Kool & the Gang comes dancing through our outdoor speaker. She may be huffing from the effort of climbing the hill, but that doesn't stop her from doing a little shimmy. I laugh, and she does a spin before flopping down on the bench across from me.

Tūtū has asthma, so she can get out of breath when

she's been working hard or the weather shifts. I listen for a whistle when she inhales, a sign her asthma is acting up, but don't hear one. That's good. In another minute, her breathing returns to normal.

"Hard work out there," she says. "Wish we had more help."

"If we lived in Arizona, we wouldn't have to do all this farming."

"You go live in Arizona, then. I stay with the family already." She pulls a couple of mountain apples from her shorts' pocket and bites into one. "Farming," she mumbles under her breath, annoyed I've used that word.

"Not farming," I say, apologetic.

She smiles and hands me the other apple.

For Hawaiians, loʻi are special because we believe that Hāloa, the first taro, is our older sibling. So when we tend our kalo, we're also caring for our family. It's not farming as much as cultivating relationship with our ancestors, our environment, and one another.

"Anyway, I can't leave you," I tell her. "Not when you're still learning to dance."

"Auwē! I dance good, Sassy. You the one no can feel the beat." Tūtū lifts her arms and swings them over her head. Now we both laugh.

I don't mind working in the lo'i. I enjoy how the water in the 'auwai makes a giggling noise and how the warm mud squishes between my toes. I like singing to the kalo, and I like that I understand how the land nourishes me. It's just that, sometimes, I feel overwhelmed by all the work Tūtū and I have to do. For example, our plan for the weekend is to harvest two taro patches and plant another. Plus, Tūtū wants us to steam and pound the taro we plan on keeping, before selling the rest to a family of poi pounders in Waialua. When Dad was here to help, it was one thing. But these days that's a lot for Tūtū and me to handle alone.

"Huu-ee," Tūtū says to catch my attention when the song ends. "I tired."

"Me too."

"Why you so tired?" She eyes me. Ever since the stuff with Leo, Tūtū's been extra attentive when I sound down.

"Just a long day. But I talked to this new girl, Pua, on the bus this afternoon and she doesn't seem so bad. She invited me over this weekend."

"Can go if you want."

"We have a lot to do here."

"Then invite her for come here."

"I don't know." Our house is really small. There's only Tūtū and me, no parents to greet a potential friend. Leo's the only person I've ever had over. "What would we do here?"

"I can put you two to work in the lo'i."

I roll my eyes. "I'm sure she'd love that."

"Never know." And then, as if she can read my mind, Tūtū adds, "Anyway, the outside is big. Good to be in this yard, beneath the trees. Special, this space."

Tūtū is right about that. Even on the days I most wish to go to Arizona, I'm still amazed by how beautiful this yard is. I bet Pua would see that, too, and love it as I do. She did like my puns, after all. She can't be so bad. "I'll ask tomorrow if she doesn't mind hanging in the lo'i."

"If she says no, can plan for one different weekend."

A different weekend?! By then she'll have found different friends. Or heard more stories about how I'm a loner. "What if she says she doesn't want to get together on another weekend?"

"You really think that going happen? She asked you over. Gotta trust people at some point. Just 'cause one thing happened with a friend, doesn't mean everything always going for go wrong."

Maybe Tūtū's right. Pua's the one who sat next to me on the bus, and who asked about my drawing, and who gasped at all the right moments when I told my Leo story. She's the one who even noticed that huge bird soaring over us. Plus, she's still new to the islands. I wonder if she's ever tried a mountain apple fresh from the tree or listened to the water in an ʻauwai tumble its way down a hill.

I look out past our garden, toward the shore. Sometimes, when a storm is brewing, the ocean is gray with thin white lines—whitewash from the big waves. On other afternoons, like today, sailboats cut across the ocean, their bright sails like spying a flock from a distance. I think again of the bird I saw out there this afternoon.

"I may have a new bird to draw," I tell Tūtū. "I saw this big one hovering above the Foodland parking lot. I didn't recognize it."

"How big?"

"Huge wingspan. Forked tail. It had a white chest but was otherwise black."

"Sounds like an ʻiwa. The great frigate bird."

"I've never seen one in your garden before."

"Good reason. ʻIwa like stay flying for weeks, never coming down to earth. Some folks say if you see one over land, a storm is nearby."

I look up into the perfectly blue sky. "I think that ʻiwa got the wrong memo."

"Animals, plants. They know things we don't. Just have to learn how for hear them."

When I was little, Papa used to tell me that instead of a green thumb, Tūtū had a green ear. She could hear what plants needed to grow. This was how she came to run a nursery dedicated to growing native plants and finding habitats for them. One of the groups she worked with even restored habitats in Pūpūkea Forest Reserve, right above our house. When Dad was a kid, he used to go up there with Tūtū all the time to clear invasive vines and bushes. They planted sandalwood and koa trees, and they tended to them so they could survive and thrive. Now Tūtū doesn't get around so easily, so I don't get to go hiking in the reserve unless Dad is in town.

"Eh," Tūtū says to attract my attention. "Your dad sent you something. Go get those boxes on the everything table." That's what we call our dining table. It's covered with my homework, Tūtū's quilting projects, mail that needs sorting, and bills that need paying. The everything table is so full that we never have room to eat there. We use the picnic table instead.

I find two boxes on the everything table. Neither is very big, but one is heavy for its size. Since he moved to Arizona, Dad has sent me gifts special to where he now lives. Prickly pear cactus candy. A poster of the Grand Canyon. He even whittled me a roadrunner because he knows how much I love birds.

"Well?" Tūtū says when I return to the lānai.

"Let's see what Dad sent this time." I tear the tape off the heavier box. Inside I find a bunch of wooden rectangles packed together like a Jenga set. "They're basswood blanks. Dad uses these to whittle."

"Open da kine," Tūtū urges me. "The other one."

In the second box, I find a set of three knives wrapped in a leather pouch. The first knife has a straight edge and is for rough cutting the wood to create a general shape. The second knife is shorter with a leaner tip and is used for detail work. The final knife looks a little like a hook and is called a chip knife. Beneath the knives is a pair of cut-resistant gloves and a book.

Over the summer, when I was with Dad and Steph in Phoenix, he taught me how to whittle a spoon, a turtle, and a bear that ended up looking like a snowman. "This is cool, but it doesn't seem especially Arizona," I say. When I reach for the book, however, a little slip of paper comes fluttering out. It's a note from Dad:

Carving out a new future for us. Can't wait to tell you everything. Love, Dad.

I snort a little. *Carving out a future.* I blame him for my

23

pun making. It must run in the family. I hand the note to Tūtū.

"You think you know what he like tell?" she asks after she's read it.

"Maybe he's ready for me to move to Phoenix!"

"Maybe," she says in a voice meant to sound chipper. Her eyes are sad, though. "Go call him for find out."

Four

"I'M HAPPY THE BOXES ARRIVED!" Dad says as he walks through his and Steph's apartment. I've video called so I can see everything Dad sees. He strolls down the hall-way, where family photos decorate the wall. There's one of Steph's parents and younger sister. One of Leo's parents with Mom and Dad. And then there's a bunch of Dad, Steph, and me from this summer.

"Tūtū is here," I tell him, swiveling the phone so Dad can see her.

"Hi, son," Tūtū says, waving.

"Hi, Mom. I'm happy you're here for this call."

"Why's that?"

"Give me a sec," Dad says. "You still there, Clara?"

I turn the screen to face me again. In the living room,

Steph is curled up on the couch with a blanket over her lap. Behind her are huge windows, with city lights sparkling in the background. "Hi, Clara," Steph says. "What's new on your end?"

"I got the gift. Thank you!"

"The tools and blanks are from your dad, but the book was my idea."

"That's really nice of you." I like Steph, so I don't tell her when she strikes out. But the truth is, I'm not great with diagrams and maps. There's something about how a 3D action looks in a 2D picture that messes with my brain. Dad says it's ironic because I'm so good at drawing, but I don't try to explain things with my drawings. I just draw what I see. This is the total opposite of Steph. She's an architectural drafter, so it's her job to make technical drawings based on architectural designs for buildings. People make what she draws.

Steph and Dad have been together for almost a year. They met right after he moved to Arizona. The wild thing is, she actually grew up on Maui, so she and Dad have a lot in common. Dad is a construction manager, and when he got this really good contract in Arizona, it was supposed to be a temporary gig. Only six months. But then his company offered him a second six-month contract, and he stayed on. He said he was building a nest egg for us, but I know at least part of him wanted to see where things went with Steph. Now, the longer he stays in Arizona, the more I miss him, and the more I feel like he's creating a whole life without me. That's another reason I have to get myself to Arizona.

"Your note said something about the future . . ." I nudge Dad.

He settles onto the couch and rests his hand on Steph's knee. "We have some big news for you."

"You're ready for me to move in with you?"

"Soon. I'm working on it."

"Okay . . ." If he's not ready for me to move, then what news could there be?

Dad and Steph scrunch their faces together so I can see both of them on the screen. They're grinning really big. "Your dad proposed!" Steph exclaims, and holds up her hand to the camera. There's a ring on her finger, as twinkly as the lights outside their window.

When I don't say anything, Dad adds, "And Steph said yes."

"Oh," I manage. "That's cool." I know I should be happy. Steph is kind and caring, not only to Dad but to me, too. Still, I feel disappointed. And left out. I can't believe Dad didn't tell me he was going to propose. We tell each other everything.

The one thing that makes me feel better is the expression on Tūtū's face. Her eyebrows fly so high up her forehead that they look ready to leap off her face. She forces them down, heaves herself up from the opposite bench, and comes to stand behind me. "Ho'omaika'i!" she says brightly. "You decide where you like get married?"

"In Hawai'i," Steph says. "Though we haven't decided between Maui or O'ahu yet."

"You folks have plenty family on both islands, so either be one good choice."

"You really wouldn't mind if the wedding was on Maui, Mom?" Dad asks.

"Not at all. Steph's the bride. Gotta keep her parents happy, too."

Dad raises his eyebrows but doesn't say anything. I get why he's surprised by Tūtū's easygoing attitude. Things have been tense between them for the past few months. Tūtū was cool when Dad planned to be in Arizona for a short time, and she was happy when he started dating a local girl. But when he extended his contract last spring, Tūtū wasn't thrilled. And things really took a turn when I said I wanted to move to Arizona. Ever since, Tūtū's been mad at Dad for going there in the first place. Now she's on a mission to get him back on Oʻahu permanently. She knows that if he's here, then I will be, too.

"If you folks going for get married here," Tūtū says, all innocent, "then where you planning for live?" There it is! The million-dollar question.

"That's a conversation we need to have," Dad says, slow and careful. "Actually, even though my current contract is almost up, a different company offered me a permanent position. I know Clara has said she wants to move to Phoenix and I was thinking—"

"Yes!" I interrupt. "I can live there with you!"

Dad laughs. "Okay, then," he says. "We will take that into consideration."

"Cannot go make one big decision off that, but," Tūtū says.

"We're not making the decision yet," Dad says. "We just want to know how Clara would feel about the possibility of a more permanent move. Maybe next summer, after the wedding."

"How about me?" Tūtū asks. "What about how I going for feel?"

"I know you love having Clara close, but I've got to think about what's best for everyone."

"It's one thing go off island as an adult, go explore and learn and come back. It's another thing take a keiki away from this land."

"I'm not considering this decision lightly, Mom. But business is booming in Phoenix, and it could be a good opportunity for us."

"Business can boom here. And who's this 'us'? I not part of the 'us'?"

"The world isn't like when you and Dad were young. Hawai'i is more expensive; the jobs off island pay better."

"Don't you get me started on how your dad and I had to scrimp and save—"

"Tūtū," I interrupt. I've seen how this argument plays out. She'll talk about how hard life was for her folks, how lucky we are to own our home, and how Dad doesn't appreciate what he grew up with. He'll say that he does appreciate it, but wants something for himself, something that he made by himself. And that will set Tūtū off on how Dad is a stubborn mule. But if I distract them, they can't argue. "I want Dad to show me how to use the gifts he got me."

Tūtū looks at me and sighs. "All right, Shrub," she says, apologetic. She turns back to the phone, to Dad and Steph. "We going for talk later, then."

"If it helps, Auntie," Steph says, "I don't want to spend a lifetime away from home."

Tūtū grumbles. "For you, five, ten years feel like nothing. But ten years *is* a lifetime for a child. They become one adult you wait too long. And ten years can be a lifetime for a grandparent, too." Tūtū hands the phone to me and heads inside, letting the screen door *thwap* behind her.

"Sorry about that, Clara," Dad says. "Tūtū and I both want the best for you, even if we don't see eye to eye on what that is."

Dad and I talk for a little while longer. He tells me to send him pictures as I work on my whittling skills. At the end of the call, we press our noses to the screen and inhale. "Aloha au iā 'oe," Dad says.

"Ha'o au iā 'oe," I reply.

By the time I hang up, the sun has already slipped behind the mountains, and in the east the color of the sky deepens quickly—in a matter of minutes it's gone from bright pink to delicate lavender to night blue. In Phoenix, the sunset is different. The pinks and oranges can linger for close to an hour.

When I move to Arizona, everything will change. The sunset, the sky, the feel of the air on my skin. The birds.

I can't wait. No one will know me as Baby Mouse. Everyone will think it's cool I'm coming from Hawai'i. I'll make friends with ease.

... Or will I? I think of Pua on the bus today. She's not having an easy time. And I haven't made it any better.

Tūtū comes back outside and stands behind me, her hands resting warm on my shoulders. "You sure quiet," she says.

"I'm just thinking."

"About your dad?"

"And moving."

"Be careful what you wish for, Shrub. Things don't always work out the way we think they will." Tūtū pauses, like there's something else she wants to say but doesn't know how. Then she shakes her head, releasing whatever thought was there. "You like eat?"

Five

TŪTŪ CHOPS VEGETABLES WHILE I spread my homework across the everything table. This year I'm taking a Hawaiian language class, and I'm struggling with the grammar. I know a lot of individual words, like *poi* or *mālama* or *loʻi*, but I don't know how to string them together to make a sentence. Sometimes sixth grade feels like this. You know there are moments that matter, but you have no idea what they'll lead to when you put them all together.

While the vegetables simmer, Tūtū joins me at the table. ʻŌlelo Hawaiʻi was still banned in schools when Tūtū was a girl, so she never got to learn it. Now she likes to practice with me.

"Koʻu pahi," I say, pointing to one of my new whittling knives.

"E holoi ʻia ka pahi," Tūtū replies, winking at me.

"Wait, what kind of word is *holoi*?"

"A verb." Tūtū points to the next chapter in the book, all about household activities.

"No fair. Now you can tell me to clean up in two different languages."

Tūtū laughs. At least she's back to her old self after the phone call with Dad.

After dinner, it's my job to holoi the dishes while Tūtū folds laundry on the lānai. When I'm finished, I pull out one of the basswood blanks that Dad sent. What should I try whittling first? I wander through the house looking for inspiration.

In the kitchen, I check out Tūtū's wooden ladle, but it's basically an oversized spoon and I made one of those already. In the dining room, I study a carving of a whale tail that Dad made. It's stunning, oiled to a soft gleam, but too advanced for me. Finally, I turn to the hallway cabinet where Tūtū keeps our family heirlooms: my great-grandpa's Purple Heart, Dad's high school diploma. And there, behind photos of uncles and aunties and cousins, I spot our ʻumeke. Carefully I open the glass door and extract it.

"What you up to?" Tūtū calls from the lānai.

34

"Nothing," I call back.

I'm not supposed to touch the 'umeke unless Tūtū is with me. The wooden bowl is a family heirloom, passed down for more generations than even Tūtū can count. Every few weeks she pulls it out of the cabinet and shows me how to oil and care for it. She even talks to it, as if it's a real live thing. Sometimes she lets me hold it. "You can ask this 'umeke any question," she says. "But the answer could surprise you."

Over the years I've asked it a lot of questions. *How old are you? Who made you? Was Tūtū kolohe when she was younger?* I've gotten some giggles out of Tūtū but never an answer from the 'umeke.

I carry the 'umeke back to my bedroom and set it on my desk. "'Umeke, what should I carve?" I ask it.

No answer. That's okay.

I grab the whittling book that Steph got me and thumb through it. There are a few really cool bird designs. A horse, which would be fun. In the section on kitchen things, there's a plate and cup. And a bowl, too. It looks a little like Tūtū's 'umeke. Except a bowl doesn't have a lid, and this 'umeke does.

Which gets me to thinking. There are a lot of different kinds of 'umeke. They can be made from gourds or wood.

35

They can store food or drink. They can have lids or not. But when 'umeke hold poi, they have a special power. When the lid is off and the poi is exposed, no one in the family can argue. To raise voices and bicker would be an insult to Hāloa, our older relative. When the lid is closed again, you can do things you wouldn't do in the presence of your elders. Like play tricks on your cousins or siblings.

So, maybe, if I carve an 'umeke and fill it with poi and leave it uncovered, then Tūtū and Dad won't be able to argue. They'll have to agree with each other. And if that happens, then I can go to Arizona.

I set to work. I try to freehand some cut lines on the basswood block, but that idea quickly goes out the window. I have no idea how to represent 3D cuts on a 2D surface. So I turn back to the book. Maybe Steph was onto something with her part of the gift. Without help, mistakes are easy to make.

The book tells me to use tracing paper to copy the design in the book. After that I can transfer the design from the paper to the basswood block, and then I'll have my cut lines. I erase my original pencil lines on the basswood and get out some tracing paper.

As I sketch the design, I think again of Dad and Steph's big announcement. Have they told Steph's parents already?

Is Dad going to tell Mom? And why, oh why, didn't he talk to me before he proposed to Steph? Why didn't he think of how all this might affect the rest of us? As much as I want to move to Arizona—and I *do* want to start over—I also get why Tūtū is upset at Dad. It isn't fair when someone is making life-changing decisions and doesn't even ask how you feel.

"Do you think it's fair?" I ask the ʻumeke.

It doesn't reply.

Carefully, I lift up its lid and peek inside. The scent is mild and woodsy. It's the scent of time and memory. I notice that someone has carved a word into the lip of the lid. It's such a tiny script that I struggle to make out the letters, but then I realize it's in Hawaiian. *Lohepono.* "Lohe" means *to listen.* I know that from class. And pono means to do something right or well. So I obey the ʻumeke and hold the opening to my ear and listen.

I'm amazed! The air trapped in there makes a noise. It sounds like the wash of waves in a seashell. Or a thousand murmuring voices in a school cafeteria. Or the rush of milk over a sketchbook.

My stomach drops. I pull the ʻumeke away from my ear.

Sometimes this happens. I'll be thinking of totally different things and then something reminds me of the beginning of the school year, and it all comes rushing back. My mind spins out. My heart feels heavy.

It still bothers me that Leo never apologized for ruining my sketchbook. And he never told Brandon or the rest of them to stop calling me names. And he never invited me to eat with him again. But what upsets me the most, even more than all those other things, is that I don't know *why*.

Why didn't Leo ever apologize? Why didn't he stand up for me? Why did he stop being friends with me? Was he tired of hanging out at Tūtū's? Was I no longer cool enough for him? Was I not as fun as his new group of friends? I don't have any answers.

"'Umeke, what are boys thinking?" I ask. And then, for good measure, I decide to ask in 'ōlelo Hawai'i. I close my eyes. "E ho'olohe mai ia'u. He aha ka mana'o o nā keikikāne?" I caress the smooth wood and wait for something to happen.

But of course, nothing does.

When I open my eyes again, the wooden bowl still gleams, as beautiful and calm as ever. I place the lid back on top and cradle the whole thing. I can imagine generations of ancestors surrounding me, and that at least is a nice feeling.

"Clara," Tūtū calls out from the kitchen. "Where you?"

"In here!" I call back.

A moment later she peeks into my room. "Eh!" she exclaims. She rushes over and grabs the 'umeke from my arms. "That's not for touch."

"I was being super careful."

"You went open the lid?"

"No," I lie.

"Well, no take it without telling me, okay?"

"Okay, sheesh, I won't."

Tūtū perches on the edge of my bed with the 'umeke in her lap. She seems calmer now that she's holding it. "Why you went get this out?"

"I wanted to use it as inspiration. To whittle my own."

"Your own?" Tūtū smiles finally. "What you need one 'umeke for?"

"To keep you and Dad from arguing."

"Oh, Shrub, I know it's hard. But even when he drives me lōlō, I love your dad. He's my son. Always." She beckons to me, and I go and sit beside her on my bed. She wraps her arm around me. "You like me tell you one story?"

"Whenever you say you like tell me one story, you mean you like teach me one lesson."

Tūtū smiles. "That's a tūtū's way, you know."

I laugh. "Okay, tell me. I'm all ears."

"This moʻolelo is about one ʻiwa. Like the bird you saw today. ʻIwa are known as thieves. They go steal food from other birds."

"They sound mean."

"Not mean. More trickster kine. In ancient Hawaiʻi, stealing was one honorable profession. Getting caught was the disgrace."

"Really?"

"Really," she repeats. "Once there was a fisherman named Keaʻau who was given magic leho. He used these cowry shells for fashion one fishing lure he named Kalokuna. After all, anything important has a name.

"Anyway, these magic shells allowed the fisherman to always return with a canoe full of heʻe, enough octopus for feed his whole village. When Chief ʻUmi on the island of Hawaiʻi heard of the leho, he took the shells for himself, and the fisherman never could ask for them back because ʻUmi was the chief.

"So Keaʻau asked many thieves for try steal the shells, but none could. Finally, Keaʻau came here, to the windward side of Oʻahu, and met the boy thief ʻIwa, whose namesake was the ʻiwa bird. That boy, he was the most talented thief. Fast and quiet and akamai. He was the only one who could steal the leho from Chief ʻUmi. And he did."

"So Kea'au got his magic shells back?"

"Not quite. Chief 'Umi had 'Iwa steal them back again." Tūtū laughs. "Poor Kea'au. No winning, yeah. Over time, Chief 'Umi had 'Iwa steal many things for him, and when the boy was ready to return home, Chief 'Umi rewarded him with a canoe full of special gifts. My tūtū used to even say that this 'umeke was one of those gifts."

I look at the 'umeke in Tūtū's lap. I imagine it nestled in a canoe, traveling across the water between islands.

"Does that mean we're descended from the boy thief 'Iwa?"

"I like for think so. I never know for sure, but my tūtū wahine, she never teach me or my brother 'ōlelo. She never teach us our mo'okū'auhau, so we never learn how for say our genealogy. Not her fault. My kūpuna, they were afraid we get in trouble in school or be kept from opportunities. That's how it was back then. Plus, my tūtū kāne died young. These are the ways knowledge gets lost. Get hard to regain. Not impossible. Just hard. And then people move away."

"Like to Arizona?"

"Like to Arizona." Tūtū cups my chin in her right hand. In her left arm still rests the 'umeke. "You make me one promise."

"What, Tūtū?"

"You promise me you no make one decision 'cause you want for run away. You make a decision because you want for go *toward* something."

Tūtū leans her forehead to mine.

"I can promise that," I say. And I want to mean it.

Six

THAT NIGHT I DREAM OF voices. Laughing voices, crying voices. High-pitched ones and low-toned ones. Breathy, anxious voices and confident voices, booming in my ears. When I awake, I don't remember any of the words that were said, just the sense that many people were speaking.

Tūtū has told me before that dreams can carry messages, but I don't know how to interpret them. So, I sit down at my desk and study the wooden blank I want to use for my 'umeke. One day it would be cool to carve something out of a native Hawaiian wood, like sandalwood, koa, or milo. But for now, basswood. By the time Tūtū knocks on my door to tell me to get ready for school, I've made my first chip. Reluctantly, I put down my knife and peel off the gloves.

After I dress, I eat oatmeal standing at the kitchen

counter while Tūtū sips coffee and fusses over me. "You remember your homework? You need wash out that water bottle? You cold this morning? Better bring a jacket."

"Yes, yes, fine," I answer, but I'm smiling. Fussing is one of the ways Tūtū shows her love.

After breakfast, I follow Tūtū's directions. All my homework goes into my school binder. My water bottle gets washed and refilled. I even stuff a windbreaker into my backpack. Then Tūtū drives me down to the Foodland parking lot to wait for the school bus. A couple of kids are lingering in their parents' cars, while the rest wait outside, chatting in pairs or groups of three. To the east, over the ocean, the sky is rosy, without a single cloud to mar the view.

"Eh, Shrub, you went get that jacket?" Tūtū asks.

"I got it." It's muggy and still, worse even than yesterday afternoon. I can't imagine I'll need any additional layers.

She tilts her head back and waggles her fingers like she's picking up signals from the sky. "Storm's coming. Tūtū knows."

"You look like you're trying a new disco move, not reading the future. Gotta go like this." I put my fingers to my temples and squint my eyes.

"You boring, Shrub. Better for sell it. Make folks

44

believe." She shakes her whole body, until the cab of the truck trembles with her. "Huu-ee! Plenty rain coming. And waves the size of mountains. I never see it like dis."

I scowl. "You serious now or you pretending?"

She smiles tenderly and brings her hand to her chest. "The way your tūtū feels, might be waves big enough for make the Eddie go." The Eddie is a big-wave-surfing contest that's only held in years when the waves top twenty feet in Waimea Bay. Usually, the energy of those huge waves is generated far to the north of us, during winter storms off the coast of Alaska. Tūtū is like a barometer. She feels weather shifts in her body.

I rest my hand on her knee. "You better take it easy."

"Or what you do, sistah?"

"I do what you do when I'm sick: tell you stay in bed or else."

She chuckles. "You too much. Go already."

I hop out of the truck and hustle to board before Kumu Maka closes the bus door. "You doing okay, Clara?" they ask as I climb the steps.

In Hawaiian, "maka" means *eyes*, and Kumu Maka's are the biggest and brownest. They train them on me now. They're always checking in on us kids, and more than once

45

they've told Brandon to stop with the Mouse stuff. So, they're basically my hero.

I spot Pua waving and pointing to the empty seat next to her. Today, for the first time in a while, I feel pretty good.

"Pua's saved a seat for me," I tell Kumu Maka.

Their worried brow relaxes. "He makamaka, ke pā la kāhea," they say.

I tilt my head, trying to figure out the translation. "The friend calls out?"

"That is a friend who calls out an invitation."

"Oh, I like that 'ōlelo no'eau."

"It's a good proverb for you right now," they agree. Kumu Maka always has wise thoughts. This is why we address them as "kumu," or *teacher*. Plus, neither *Uncle* nor *Auntie* would fit right. Kumu Maka is māhū, with elements of both kāne and wahine.

As soon as I sit down, I ask Pua, "Where's your uke?"

"Under the seat."

"You have to keep it in your lap, or the boys will take it again." I reach down for it. "Here, rest it across both our knees. Now it's really safe."

There are a handful of other kids already on the bus. The boys' voices seem louder than usual, with snippets of conversation buzzing back and forth.

46

"Did you talk to your tūtū?" Pua asks. "About coming over this weekend?"

"Um, yeah. We have a lot of work to do so I can't go over to anyone's house."

"Oh," Pua says softly.

"But you could come over to our place. I mean, if you want to work outside. It's not much of an offer, I know. But we have to harvest our loʻi."

"Wait, loʻi like a taro patch? You actually have one?"

"More than one."

"That's so cool. Poi is my favorite food. When we lived in Seattle, I even brought poi once for show-and-tell."

"How'd that go?"

"Most of my friends were willing to try it."

"Wow. When we lived in Kansas, my classmates thought poi was an alien creature."

"What were you doing in Kansas?"

"My mom was stationed there. I lived a lot of places before my parents divorced."

"And now you want to move again?"

I shrug. I don't want to move necessarily. I just have to get out of here.

"Where'd you find poi in Seattle?" I ask, trying to change the subject.

"Sometimes one of the specialty Asian grocery stores would get it in stock. Then my parents filled our freezer with it."

"So you've never had it fresh?"

Pua shakes her head.

"Oh, you don't even know, then." Store-bought poi is usually dull gray, without much flavor. If it's been frozen before shipping, then the poi clumps together and resembles paste. But homemade poi is nothing like that.

"Know what?" Pua's eyes get big.

"Fresh poi is sweet. It tastes like mountain water. And our kind has a pinkish note, which makes it so pretty. I like mine real smooth. Two-finger poi. But my dad likes it thick. One-finger poi. For his birthday last year, Tūtū express-mailed him a whole box of our pa'i 'ai so he could add the water himself. It's the water that makes poi sour so you don't want to add it until you're ready to eat. My dad said it was the best gift he could have gotten."

"Your dad must miss Hawai'i a lot."

I shrug. "I don't know. When he was with my mom, he did. But with Steph—that's his fiancée—he seems pretty happy on the mainland."

"My parents tried for years to find a way back here. We were lucky when the university hired my mom."

The bus huffs to the stop in Hale'iwa. Denny and Leo high-five Kumu Maka as they board. I'm about to ask Pua more about her mom's job when Denny comes strutting down the aisle. "I HOPE SOMEONE NOTICES MY NEW KICKS!"

Could Denny be any louder? I'm surprised no one else turns his way. Of course, I look at his shoes, and I have to admit they're worth admiring—bright red basketball lace-ups with these space-age foam soles. "Come on, come on," Denny mumbles. "Someone notice."

Not a single person looks up.

By the time Denny reaches our row, he's crestfallen. Sure, he can be annoying, but I'd want someone to say something if I was wearing those shoes.

"Sweet dunks," I say.

"Thanks, eh." He gives me a big genuine smile. "Great shirt."

I glance down. I'm wearing my favorite T-shirt, one Dad got me as an Arizona gift. It's a picture of a cactus and the words, *I'm prickly*. Another great pun. I wear it at least once a week, and no one has ever commented on it before.

Pua must have me feeling confident, because when I see Leo glancing at my shirt, I smile at him.

I hear him say, "Ha! Prickly. I get it."

"I bet you've agreed with my shirt for a long time." I expect Leo to chuckle. Maybe I even think that making a joke at my own expense will lead him to talk to me more.

Instead, he looks totally confused. "Huh? What are you talking about?"

"You know, how I can be like a cactus."

"I never said that." Leo frowns.

"I can be prickly," I try again.

"I don't know what you're talking about." Leo looks right at me. *Why does Clara act like I'm always dissing her?* I'm staring at his face, but his mouth never moves. It's like he's a ventriloquist.

"I don't act like that," I say.

Is this a trick or something? Leo's lips are clamped shut in a tight line, but his voice is clear and strong. I'm too stunned to say anything more, and after a second, he heads toward the back of the bus.

"Wow, I didn't expect you to beef with Leo first thing in the morning," Pua says.

"I didn't beef. I thought he liked my shirt, so I made a joke about it."

"It was Denny who complimented your shirt."

"Sure, and then Leo."

"I don't know about that." Pua shrugs. She's distracted by the view of all the little shops that line Hale'iwa's main street.

Around me voices surge. "Pua," I say, tapping her on the shoulder. "Did you hear Denny say anything when he got on the bus?"

"We just went over this. He said something about your shirt."

"No, before that."

"You told him you liked his shoes."

"And before that?

She gives me a look like I'm talking nonsense. "He didn't say anything." She claps her hands on her 'ukulele case. "After yesterday, I was watching every move he made."

I believe her, and yet I heard Denny. I know I did! But how?

I glance around me. Who else can I hear? Not Pua. She's staring out the window in silence. Not Gigi or Nahele, the fifth graders sitting in front of me. They're working quietly on long division.

I look around for someone else, and spot Titus. On the bus he barely speaks—all his friends live near school or ride other buses—and he always has his nose in a book.

It does not do to leave a dragon out of your calculations, I hear him say aloud. Or read aloud? Or think? Is that even possible? I'm not sure anymore.

The voices are still surging. *Did I finish my homework? . . . I hope it's sloppy joe day in the cafeteria. . . . I wish we could bring dogs to school. . . . My sister better not be in my room right now!*

What is happening?!?!

I'm reminded of my dream, all those voices filling my head. Am I still asleep? If I pinch myself, will I wake up? I grab a piece of skin on my left arm and squeeze. "Ouch!"

"Are you okay?" Pua asks.

"Yeah, of course. I'm totally normal."

She gives me a funny look before turning back to the window.

A red light touched the points of standing rocks. Titus's voice intrudes again. His lips are closed, his eyes on his book. *The dragon came.*

I know he's not saying anything aloud, yet I also know I'm hearing exactly what's in his head.

How can this be happening?

Can I really hear what he's thinking? What *all* these boys are thinking?

Seven

"HELLO! EARTH TO CLARA!" PUA snaps her fingers in my face to get my attention. She just asked me something about Tūtū's garden but I don't know what. Boys' voices are drowning out everything else!

I put my head between my knees and smash my hands over my ears. This muffles what the boys are saying out loud—because I can hear that, too, of course—but nothing stops me from hearing their thoughts.

I wonder how many marshmallows I can fit in my mouth. . . . I forgot my PE clothes! . . . No dragon can resist the fascination of riddling talk and of wasting time trying to understand it.

"Are you okay?" Pua looks worried.

"I think I might be sick."

"Is it a headache? Is that why you're holding your head like that?"

I nod, but it's no headache. Headaches don't make you read people's minds. Nothing can make you read someone's mind. So what is going on?

I try pinching myself again. I try humming Kool & the Gang songs. I try anything that might make the voices go away. But nothing helps. If anything, the voices get louder. Finally, I dig my fingers into Pua's 'ukulele case and make myself white-knuckle the rest of the bus ride. Once we get to school, things will have to return to normal. I'll walk off the bus and the voices will disappear. Or I'll wake up from this dream. Or something will happen to make the world right again.

When at last the bus parks in front of our school, I can't wait to get out of there. I stumble down the steps and lean against the school gate. Sixth, seventh, and eighth graders flood past me, eager to join their friends or head to class.

Only Pua stays behind. "I can take you to the nurse's office," she says tentatively.

"Yeah, that's really nice. I think, maybe . . ." But as suddenly as the voices filled the bus, they trail off. It's over. Quiet!

"Hey, you two okay?" Kumu Maka calls out to us.

"We're fine." I manage a wan smile.

"Then hele on to class."

"Going right now!" Pua waves as Kumu Maka closes the bus door.

Whatever was going on in the bus is gone now. Maybe I was hallucinating. Or maybe the boys were talking more than usual. Because there's no way I was actually hearing their thoughts. Whatever it was, it's over now. It has to be.

But as Pua and I cross the soccer field to the school's side entrance, I pick up whispers. *Gotta finish this reading before homeroom. . . . I hope my auntie brings me back something cool from her trip. . . . Why is bacon so 'ono?*

By the time we reach the hallway, the whispers have turned into a full-on cacophony. Pua leaves me to retrieve books from her locker, and I try to focus on my own locker combination. But there are too many voices—as if a thousand mynah birds are screeching at once.

I mash my hands over my ears. It's fruitless! What else can I do? Scream? Cry? Tell every single boy to stop thinking?

I crouch to the ground. That's how Pua finds me. "Are you sure you don't want to go to the nurse?" Her voice manages to cut through all the noise. I shake my head no. Instead, I grab her sleeve and drag her toward my homeroom. If I can get to a classroom without kids, I might be okay. Pua, however, resists.

Okay, sure, her homeroom is on the other side of school, but that is not the point. She pulls one arm away from me, so I grab on to the other. I'm like a piece of packing tape she can't get rid of. Finally, she manages to deposit me in front of my homeroom. "What is going on?" she asks.

I've got to pull it together. "I'm overwhelmed by all the talking." I bare my teeth against the onslaught of noise.

"Oh!" Pua's eyes get big. "Was I talking a lot on the bus? I can do that sometimes."

I want to say it's not her who's talking too much, but just then a group of boys walks by. "Later," I manage to squeak, and I make a run for it. The last I see of poor Pua is her standing alone in the middle of the hall.

When I duck into the classroom, Kumu Whitman is writing on the whiteboard. He teaches sixth-grade science, and he's my favorite teacher, so I'm lucky to have him for homeroom, too.

"G'day, Clara, aloha kakahiaka," he says as I take my seat. Kumu Whitman has a shock of bright red hair and speaks with an Australian accent. Sometimes he brings us Australian snacks, like Cheezels, which taste like Cheetos but are shaped into fat rings. Even though he didn't grow up here, he's always working on learning more 'ōlelo Hawai'i. He says it's good for him as a teacher and as a malihini noho loa.

"Hi, Kumu." I wait for his thoughts to bombard me, but all I get is silence. Wonderful, beautiful, perfect silence. At last! I melt into my chair.

I pull out my school planner and gel pens. As part of homeroom, we have to record the day's bulletin, so I like to make it fun by adding sketches. Now that things are quiet again, I can go back to normal. I draw a tree, each branch a line where I add a new announcement.

A couple of girls arrive and settle into their seats. On the whiteboard Kumu Whitman notes that our school library is hosting an art contest called Anywhere in the Worlds. The directions are to represent a place we'd like to visit. We can draw, collage, sculpt, or use whatever material we want. The place can be anywhere, from a fantastical world we'd find in a book to somewhere real. The directions are pretty open. Immediately I'm thinking of the Grand Canyon and how beautiful it was this summer. Or maybe New York City, which I want to see one day.

But before I can hear more about the contest, the racket starts up again. Two boys are talking about a TV show they watched last night. Another is memorizing lyrics to a rap song. Ollie, who is Titus's best friend, is next to me, and he must be reading the same book as Titus because I feel like I'm getting the continuation of this morning's bus ride. *Dragons may not have much real use for all their wealth, but they know it to an ounce as a rule . . .*

"Enough with the dragons!" I yell.

Ollie looks up at me, and then at Kumu Whitman. "All I was doing was reading. I swear."

Kumu Whitman frowns.

"I'm sorry. Ollie's right. I'm, um . . ." I search for an excuse for my outburst. "I'm sensitive about dragons right now."

Ollie gives me a look but goes back to his book. I, on the other hand, want to curl into a ball under my desk. Who says they're sensitive about dragons?! What is that even?

I pick at the cap to my gel pen as the last few stragglers make it to their desks before the final class bell rings. Kumu Whitman starts in on the day's announcements, but I can barely hear him. There's the audiobook to my left and the rap song behind me. One boy ate too much for breakfast and another forgot his homework or to feed his dog or maybe his homework ate his dog, I don't know, because it's all running together and—

"Oi! Clara! What are you doing?" Kumu Whitman is standing above me, his hands on his hips.

I follow Kumu Whitman's gaze to my desk. There's gel ink everywhere! I must have pulled the cap off my pen without noticing, and now my hands are an iridescent pink. Can this day get any worse?

Kumu Whitman points to the cupboard where he keeps the paper towels and spray cleaner. At least I'm in a science classroom with a ton of cleaning supplies because it takes the rest of homeroom for me to wipe up the ink. Only when I'm done do I realize that the voices faded while I was cleaning. Does spray cleaner scare them away? I try a couple more squirts, but it's no use. The voices are back.

As the bell rings for passing period and everyone packs up to go to their first-period class, Ollie pauses next to my desk. "When you're ready to tackle your dragon sensitivity," he says in an official tone, "I can recommend some good books."

"Oh, thanks," I manage.

He gives me a curt nod and heads out of the classroom, book tucked under his arm.

Because I have Kumu Whitman again for first period, I hang out in his classroom. It's peaceful in here between classes. He breaks out a Violet Crumble and offers me a piece. "My mum sent me a whole box of them."

"That's really nice."

"She's a good one, my mum," he agrees. That's what I mean about Kumu Whitman. Even though I covered a desk with pink ink, he doesn't hold it against me. The outside of the candy bar melts against the warmth of my fingers. I pop the piece into my mouth and the chocolate gives way to a crumbly center that tastes like toffee and honey. "Need another paper towel?" Kumu Whitman asks.

I get up to grab it from him. Don't want to get my desk dirty again! But as I return to my seat, I brush against Kumu Whitman's desk, knocking his old-school tie to the ground. He's talked about it before. How he keeps it on his desk to remind himself of what kind of teacher he wants to be. I bend down to pick it up.

And suddenly I'm falling.

The ground gives way and there's a long drop. My stomach flip-flops and then—

I'm in a classroom. It's like mine but different. Chalkboards instead of whiteboards. Wooden desks instead of metal and molded plastic. The computer is big and old-school and it hums loudly in the corner with its green screen.

I'm standing next to a boy with thick red hair. He's nervous. I want to ask him where I am, but I can't speak. It's like a dream, this world. I can't exactly control it but I'm part of it at the same time.

In front of us are two dark-haired boys. They're standing on either side of a podium. I realize I'm surrounded by boys. No girls in sight. The boys all wear the same uniform. Red shorts, red shirt, yellow tie.

"I'll take Matt," says the dark-haired boy to the left. He points to someone next to me, and a blond kid crosses the room.

"I'll take Geoff, then," the other dark-haired boy says. They must be choosing teams for something. I check out the chalkboards and realize that one has rules for debate. That's it! Debate team.

One by one classmates are chosen, until there's only me and the red-haired boy. "I guess we're stuck with Whitty, then," the first dark-haired boy says.

"Rather be one man down than be stuck with him," the other says with a laugh.

"We've odd numbers anyway," the teacher chimes in. "Whitty, take a seat by the window, won't you? We don't need you."

I feel the redheaded boy's embarrassment. I feel his disappointment. And I feel angry on his behalf. How can a teacher act like this?

But before I can see anything else, the world fades.

Eight

THE CLASSROOM RETURNS. I'M CLASPING a paper towel in one hand and a yellow tie in the other. The red-haired boy in my vision looked exactly like a mini Kumu Whitman. So it had to be him. But *how*? Did I travel back in time? Did I conjure a vision? Did I see his memories?

I stare down at Kumu Whitman's tie. The yellow silk seems to glow in my hand. Hurriedly I drop it back on Kumu's desk. I don't know what I can trust anymore. Maybe I should go to the nurse's office. Or hide in the janitor's closet. Or run away!

I take a step toward the classroom door. I've got to escape. But just as I grip the doorjamb, the first bell rings, warning everyone class is about to begin. Kids come streaming in, pressing me back. I collapse into my seat.

The voices are everywhere! Behind me, Denny is texting Brandon to tell him about his new shoes. Two rows over Titus is reading his book again. A few seats forward Rizal is wondering if gym socks can grow mold. (They can, I want to tell him. I know from experience.)

Pua slips into the seat across from mine. "How's your head?"

"Exploding!" I yelp.

"Whoa," Pua says, pulling back. I may have been a tiny bit intense.

"Sorry," I mumble. I need to pull it together! But how?

Then I think of Dad. How much he hates airports. He doesn't mind flying, he's quick to point out. It's only the airports. Something about crowds, the noise, the lines. So he has this trick. He counts his breath. Breathe in for five seconds, breathe out for five seconds. In for five, out for five. I close my eyes, trying to focus on the numbers I'm counting. One-two-three-four-five. And after a while, it works! The boys' voices die down to a murmur. I don't feel like making a mad dash for the farthest corner of the baseball field. The final bell rings, and I open my eyes in time to catch Michelle and Leo sliding into their seats.

"Daydreaming about Disneyland, Milky Mouse?" Michelle says. Crystal, seated behind Pua, snickers.

"She has a headache," Pua says, trying to defend me.

To my surprise, Denny steps in. "Be cool, Michelle. My mom gets migraines, and they're the worst."

For a moment, I wonder if Denny thought that or said it out loud. He's usually the first to laugh when Michelle makes fun of someone. But when she crosses her arms and pouts, I realize Denny really did stand up for me.

Kumu Whitman frowns at Denny and then points to the whiteboard. "Attention up here, everyone. Your next assignment will be a group project."

A few people turn to wave at their friends. Michelle motions to Crystal and Leo to be in a group together. Pua glances at me, and I nod back.

"You'll be happy to know," Kumu Whitman continues, "that I've chosen your groups for you." He walks between the rows of desks handing out assignment sheets.

"Why can't we choose our own groups?" Denny asks.

"I've given careful thought to these groupings, so they are final."

Denny sighs dramatically.

Kumu Whitman calls out names. Some kids smile and some high-five and some look shyly at one another, though no one's unhappy. Finally, Kumu calls my name. "Clara, you're with Denny and Titus."

Denny and Titus?! Now I wish I could read Kumu Whitman's mind. Why would he put the three of us together? If Denny has anything to contribute, it's going to be making fun of Titus and me. He's always either cracking a joke or laughing at one. I don't think I've seen him serious ever.

And Titus is the total opposite. So quiet that I can't remember the last time he said hi or even made eye contact with me. What I know about him I pick up from his friends. They're always talking about Middle-earth and Orcs and how Titus is growing out his hair to look like Legolas from *Lord of the Rings*.

But if I think I have it bad, I just have to look at Pua. She's with Leo and Michelle. The first thing Michelle does is call across the room to Crystal's partners. "We'll trade you what's-her-face for Crystal."

Pua turns bright pink. "I'm Pua," she whispers. Is she is trying to tell Michelle that, or the other group?

I wave my hand to get Kumu Whitman's attention. "We'd be happy to have Pua in our group."

"Thank you, Clara, but that's not how I made the assignments. Pua will stay with her group and Crystal with hers. Remember, I have placed you in these groups for a reason. Each of you have strengths that can build off your partners' and help all of you grow together."

I look from Denny to Titus and back to Denny again. What skills do they have that I need to grow? And what strengths do I have that these two are going to care about?

Seems they are thinking along the same lines.

Titus stares at his desk as if he wants to disappear into it. *Why did I take choir as my elective? I could have been in fourth-period science with my friends. Denny and Clara just think I'm weird.*

Denny's no happier. *Clara and Titus think I'm a joke. They're not going to listen to any of my ideas.*

I want to bury my head in my notebook. I *do* think that Titus is weird. And I *do* think Denny is the class clown. But now I can hear how the two of them are afraid of others thinking exactly that, and I feel a little bad for my own thoughts about them.

Kumu Whitman explains that our assignment is to choose a waterway like a river or stream and study a section of it. We can look at where the waterway originates in the mountains, or an area that it flows through, or where it spills into the ocean. Then we are to document which plants and animals live nearby and how they interact with one another and their water source. "You might even try to imagine what the area looked like a hundred or two hundred years ago," Kumu Whitman suggests. "All this can go into your observation journal."

This sounds like a super cool project, and I'm excited about it. But I don't know how Denny, Titus, and I will work together. We've got nothing in common.

When it's time for the groups to talk, Denny is full of ideas. "We should choose a good surf break. Like Sunset. Or Waimea Bay."

Titus doesn't reply, just hides behind a curtain of thick hair.

"I'll surf while you two do our project." Denny nudges Titus, like he knows this suggestion will annoy him.

"As if," I say. "You're definitely going to carry your weight on this. But I'm down with choosing the Waimea River."

"Don't you live up there?" Titus asks from behind his hair. "On the Waimea River?"

"We're actually on the KālunawaiKaʻala Stream. It comes out near Pūpūkea, not Waimea Bay."

"Maybe we can do our project near your place," Titus suggests quietly. "If you don't mind asking your parents?"

"My tūtū," I correct him. "She's the one I live with."

Oh no, did I insult Clara? I shouldn't have assumed

she lived with her parents. I always say the wrong thing. I shouldn't have said anything at all.

"It's okay, Titus. I don't mind asking her."

Okay. Clara said it was okay. I didn't insult her too badly.

I'm glad I could help Titus calm down. And I know Tūtū will be ecstatic for me to have classmates over. But I feel hesitant about the whole thing. Inviting Pua was a big enough deal. Now Denny and Titus? Who will it be next?

"Going to Clara's place is a great idea," Denny says enthusiastically. "Afterward we can go down to surf."

"Or maybe fish akule," Titus says. As soon as he's spoken, his thoughts get the better of him. *Bet Denny will say that's lame. I should have kept my mouth shut.*

"Let's see how the conditions are," Denny says. "If the akule go run, I like fish."

"What about me?" I ask. No way they're going to exclude me from this decision.

"Bossy pants over here," Denny says, motioning to me.

Titus chuckles into his hair. "Okay, Clara can choose what we do when the project is all pau."

"Just no lying on a towel," Denny says. "I like to do stuff." I wait for Denny to think about how boring I am, or how he wishes he was in a different group. But his thoughts merely echo what he said. *Sitting around is the worst.*

Suddenly, Michelle's voice rings out. "I don't care which river you want to study. You don't even know the differences."

We all turn to stare. Pua is blinking back tears and her lower lip is trembling. Leo is across the room at the computer, totally unaware of the drama in his group.

"You're not from here," Michelle says to Pua. "You may look local, but inside I bet you're all haole."

Crystal lets out a low, "Ooooooh."

"Those be fighting words," Denny adds.

Michelle's eyes narrow, and I know she is going in for the kill. "You're not one of us at all. And you never will be."

Nine

I FIND PUA IN THE girls' bathroom, seated on the tile floor with her forehead resting on her knees. She's breathing in little gulps of air, the way I do after I've been sobbing. Her face is flush and her eyes red-rimmed.

I pull a paper towel from the dispenser and run it under some cold water. "Here," I say, handing it to her. "Pat it on your face. It will help get rid of the red."

"I can't go back out there," she says.

"We have ten minutes until the end of the period." I sit down next to her on the cold tile floor. "So for ten more minutes we can stay here."

"I'm never leaving this bathroom," she cries. "I'll hide out in one of these stalls until the end of the day and then I'll call my mom to pick me up."

I run my hand along the green bathroom tiles. Pua has no idea how many times I've hidden out here. I understand what she's feeling, but that doesn't mean she has to go through what I did. "What happens tomorrow? And the day after? At some point you have to face the world again."

"No, I don't."

I remember saying something similar to Tūtū at the beginning of the year.

Pua drops her head onto her knees again. "I was different in Seattle, but it was cool-different. I had friends. I *belonged*. I thought coming here would be like that but better. My mom told me I'd love hanging out with my cousins, and my dad said I'd get to take 'ukulele lessons, but you know what happened? My cousins are all my brother's age and don't have time for me, and my 'ukulele lessons don't mean I'm any closer to knowing what it means to be Hawaiian. And no one here likes me or thinks I belong. You heard what Michelle said. I'm never going to fit in."

I want to tell Pua that she's wrong, that she'll fit in no problem. I want to promise her that things will get better and she'll have a whole bunch of friends eventually. But the truth is, I don't know. I don't fit in anywhere either, and I definitely don't have a bunch of friends. Pua is the first person I've hung out with since school started in August.

"I want to move back to Seattle," she sobs. When she blows her nose, the sound echoes against the bathroom walls.

I rest my arm over Pua's shoulders. "I think you belong here."

"Why?" Pua sniffles.

"You being here helps me feel like I belong more. So maybe me being here is part of why you belong, too."

"That doesn't make any sense," she says, wiping her eyes on her shirt. "But it does make me feel better. Especially after you were acting all weird this morning. I thought maybe you were trying to freak me out so I wouldn't want to come over to your place."

"I wasn't trying to scare you. I just . . . see . . ." I stumble over my words.

I don't know what to do. I want to tell Pua. But why would she ever believe me? I barely believe what's happening to me. And yet, I need help figuring out what is going on with all these boys' thoughts in my head. I need someone who will help me know what's real or not.

I take a deep breath. "What if I told you I could read boys' minds?" I say finally.

"That's a good one." Pua chuckles. "You do know how to make someone feel better."

"No, really," I protest. "What would you say if I told you that? That I can read boys' minds?"

"I'd ask why you aren't putting your superpowers to better use."

"Better use?"

"Yeah. Like if you can do that, you should have gotten Denny to hand over my 'ukulele yesterday, and you should make Titus talk to someone—anyone—on the bus."

"I said I can *read* their minds, not control them."

"In that case, I don't think it's a very good superpower." Pua stands to wash her hands.

She's right. I have a not-so-*super* power that's making me feel totally out of control, *and* I can't even do anything with it. At least superheroes can go around rescuing people or cats or leaping over really tall buildings. What can I do? Hear more about dragons?

"Unless . . ." Pua spins around to face me. She's grinning wide and has a playful glint in her eye.

"Unless what?"

"Unless you can use their thoughts against them. Like to get them to do what you want."

Could that be possible? If I could get Brandon to stop calling me names . . . Or if I could get Leo to talk to me like before . . . My heart aches a little at the thought of Leo and me actually talking again. Better to start smaller. "How would I even do that? Like, how could I get Brandon to stop calling me Baby Mouse?"

Pua taps her finger against her chin, plotting a plan. "Okay, I've got it. Let's say you hear Brandon thinking about how much he wants ice cream. So, you go to the cafeteria and buy an ice cream bar. Then you tell him you'll give him the ice cream if he does something for you. Like never call you Baby Mouse again."

I'm into Pua's idea, but it's too simple. "I don't really think Brandon would give up calling me Baby Mouse in exchange for an ice cream bar. Do you?"

"Probably not." Pua laughs. "But it's all hypothetical, so what does it matter?"

"It's *not* hypothetical!" I want Pua to understand. This isn't pretend to me. "*It's real.* And it just started today! It's why I had that headache on the bus. Why I acted so distracted. I can't turn it off. All of a sudden, boys' voices, their thoughts, are everywhere." I throw my hands into the air.

"In here? Right now?" She's smiling, and I know she thinks I'm kidding around.

"Not in the girls' bathroom. But everywhere else they're overwhelming."

"Is this like a hidden camera thing?" She peeks under the sink and around the trash can.

"I'm being totally serious. I can hear what boys are thinking." I clap my hands over my ears and squeeze shut my eyes. If I have to have this power, then at least I could use it to make my life a little more tolerable. No more nicknames. No more hiding in bathrooms. Just a peaceful existence until I move to Arizona. "Pua," I whisper, "I really need someone to believe me."

Pua gently pries my hands from my ears. When I open my eyes, she's gazing at me with sympathy. "I'll believe you," she says, "but only if you prove it to me."

Ten

FOR THE PAST TWO AND a half months, I've eaten in the bathroom or the loading zone behind the cafeteria. Today Pua leads me to one of the monkeypod trees, where the other sixth graders eat. Well, almost all the sixth graders. Michelle and her crew eat near the banyan tree, where the seventh graders usually hang out.

"Here we listen for boys," Pua says as she plops down on one of the empty benches. But, for once, there are no boys around.

"If my brother were here, you could practice on him," Pua says. "He's in ninth grade. He's not bad, as far as brothers go." While we wait for boys to show up, Pua tells me about her family. They all live in her grandparents' house.

Her dad is a chef and wants to open a restaurant of his own, and her mom is a marine biologist. It's because of her mom that Pua suggested the Kaluanui Stream to Michelle and Leo. Apparently, there are some rare mountain shrimp that can be found there. "I don't mind studying a different waterway," Pua says. "I just don't understand why Michelle insists on Waikīkī."

"It's a see and be seen place."

"She does love the spotlight." Pua nods toward the banyan tree, where Michelle is excitedly telling a story to Leo and Denny. She has Leo's undivided attention, though Denny keeps rubbing at his sneakers.

Crystal and Brandon walk by us on their way to join the others. "Look," Crystal says, "it's Baby Mouse and What's-Her-Face."

I wait for Brandon to add something snarky, and when he doesn't, I wonder if he has a gentler side, like Denny. As he draws closer, though, I hear him thinking: *Clara found a friend as weird as she is.*

Well, there goes that theory.

"You pick up anything?" Pua whispers after they've passed.

"Brandon thinks you're as weird as I am."

"I could have told you that." Pua pulls a packet of li hing mui gummy worms from her lunch bag and holds them out to me.

I pop a few of the gummy worms in my mouth. They taste like plum and lemon peel and salt. Even at this distance, I pick up murmurs of thoughts. A sixth grader doesn't want to spend the weekend at his dad's place. A kid in my Hawaiian language class is hoping for a passing grade on our latest quiz. I scoot closer to Brandon, trying to pick something up. But he's too far away. All I get are snippets of Denny's thoughts.

. . . stepping on my new shoes . . . all dirty now . . .

I scoot farther down the bench to hear better.

At least Brandon could apologize.

I slide back toward Pua. "I think I've got something. Denny wants Brandon to apologize for stepping on his shoes."

"Oooh, those are his new ones, right?"

I nod. "Denny was really excited about them on the bus."

"He's dabbing at them with a napkin right now. Something must have gone down."

"Do you think I should go over there?"

"If you're joking, stop now." Pua looks concerned. "Michelle will eat you for lunch. It's not worth some gag."

"I told you, this is real." I grab the empty gummy worm bag. "And I'm going to prove it." I head for the trash can next to the banyan tree. Behind me, Pua watches nervously.

As I reach the trash can, Brandon's voice rings out. "Hey, Baby Mouse. What's that rat's nest you got there?"

I think of what Pua said in the bathroom. How reading boys' minds could mean getting them to do what I want. And what do I want? For Brandon to stop calling me Baby Mouse. So I'm going to make him feel exactly how he's made me feel every time he's used that stupid nickname. Then he'll start to understand what it's been like.

"I know you're not insulting me," I say, turning to face him. "Not after you made a mess of Denny's shoes." *There, that should do it.*

She can't know I did that on purpose. Brandon's thought pops in the air around me.

"You stepped on them on purpose?" Okay . . . I did not see that coming.

"What?" Denny looks up. "What'd Clara say?"

Brandon's eyes get big. *I didn't mean to. Well, I did, kind of, but I feel bad about it. It's basically Denny's fault for bragging so much about them. Who does Clara think she is?*

"Dude, you said you tripped." Denny smacks Brandon on the shoulder.

79

Brandon slaps Denny's hand away. "Whatever. They were going to get dirty anyway." Brandon puffs up his chest. *Your parents will buy you a new pair.*

"Did you just slap my hand away?" Denny's face turns red. *I can't believe Brandon would lie to me.* "Are you getting up in my space? Gonna mess up something else of mine?"

Is he this mad for real? Brandon stands so he's towering over Denny. *Do his stupid shoes mean more than me?* "Maybe I'm gonna mess up your face."

I glance at Pua, who looks horrified. When I turn back around, Crystal and Michelle are frozen, totally stunned.

Denny stands up and presses his chest against Brandon's.

This is not supposed to happen.

Brandon pushes Denny.

I didn't want this!

A seventh grader yells, "Fight!"

I look at Leo, and he makes eye contact with me. Kids are pouring in from every corner of the yard. "Calm down, guys." Leo has to shout to be heard. *What just happened?*

All these people are looking. Brandon glances from side to side at the circle forming around him and Denny. *I can't back down now.*

If I don't step up, everyone will think I'm a wimp. Denny puffs up his chest and stands as tall as he can.

The circle tightens, kids chanting, "Fight! Fight! Fight!"

The crowd drowns out Leo's words. They drown out Brandon's and Denny's thoughts. I try to push my way to the center, but before I can do anything, Brandon lunges and Denny swings.

I close my eyes, not wanting to see what happens. I hear an "oof!" and a soft sound, and when I open my eyes again, Brandon is bent over, holding his stomach. In the next moment he pushes Denny to the ground. My head is so loud with voices that I want to scream.

"Disperse!" a voice calls out. "Disperse!" It's Kumu Whitman, shooing students away.

At our school you can get in trouble for encouraging a fight, so kids scramble back to their lunch benches. Denny and Brandon are grappling on the ground, but no one's trying to hit anyone anymore. Kumu Whitman and our head teacher, Kumu Apo, pull the two of them apart.

Within seconds, the big crowd has completely disappeared. Even Michelle and Crystal have stepped back to the banyan tree. Only Leo, Pua, and I remain.

"What happened here?" Kumu Apo addresses all of us. She's holding on to Brandon. Every part of his body is rigid with anger.

On the other side of Kumu Whitman is Denny, who's

glaring at Brandon's back. "One of you needs to speak up," Kumu Whitman says.

But I don't think Denny or Brandon can speak. Their thoughts are jumbled, falling over one another: *his fault . . . how could he . . . I'm gonna . . .* Only Leo is forming a full thought, and it's the same question running on repeat: *Why'd they go at each other?*

"If no one tells me what happened, I'm going to haul you all into my office," Kumu Apo warns. Then she looks at me. "Tell me the truth, Clara."

She knows I'm incapable of lying to teachers. But if I tell the whole truth, I'll have to admit to my part in all this, and she'd never believe that.

"Um . . . so, I . . . well . . . ," I stammer.

"It was a misunderstanding," Pua cuts in. "Brandon stepped on Denny's shoes, and it seemed like he did it on purpose but really it's because he's so clumsy."

Brandon shoots Pua a look that says he resents being called clumsy, but he doesn't argue with her story.

"That's what this is about?" Kumu Whitman asks incredulously. "What kind of friends fight over shoes?"

"They were my birthday present," Denny mumbles. Brandon doesn't say anything.

Kumu Apo releases a deep sigh. "Okay, Leo, Pua, and Clara, you're free to go. Brandon and Denny, we've got a long chat coming up."

The kumus escort Brandon and Denny toward the office. Even though the boys still won't look at each other, their thoughts shift. Instead of focusing on one another, now they're worried about getting in trouble.

When they disappear into the main hall, Leo turns to me. "I tried to stop them, you know." *You saw me try to stop them, right?*

"I saw you."

"I wanted to do the right thing, but everything got out of control so fast." Leo digs his fingers into his curls, his habit when he's overwhelmed. "You know I try to do right by my friends." *Like I tried to reach out to you . . .*

Reach out to me? What? "Do you mean that one text that you—?"

I can't believe those two. Fighting like that. Leo's thoughts cut my question short. He slings his backpack over his shoulder so hard that it makes a smacking sound. *I'm so over everyone right now.* Without looking back, Leo hikes it for class. He doesn't even say goodbye to Michelle and Crystal. A full ten minutes left of lunch period and

83

he's done with all of us.

Pua and I watch Leo disappear into the science building, and then she turns to me. "That is not how I thought that would go."

"Me neither." I slump onto the nearest bench. "Whatever this power is, I think I'm better off without it."

"Don't say that! You just need a little more practice."

"I don't want practice! I want to be with my dad already." I want to give up on Leo. I want to be far from Brandon and Denny. I want to get off this island!

Pua sits down next to me. "But isn't that happening already?" she asks glumly.

I think of my conversation with Dad last night. Moving to Arizona isn't happening soon enough for me. It was one thing when my life was messed up by things beyond my control. It's another thing when it's messed up because of something I did. This new power isn't helping my life. It's making it worse. Honestly, the only way this power would be useful is if it got me to Arizona sooner. And how is it going to do that?

Eleven

THE WHOLE REST OF THE school day and the bus ride home, my thoughts churn. What if my mind reading *could* get me to Arizona sooner? What if I can help Dad see that summer is too long of a wait? That moving me sooner would be good for him and me?

I keep going back to that moment with Kumu Whitman's tie, how holding it dropped me into a memory or vision. What if I could do the same thing with a belonging of Dad's? See into his memories or past? Then I might discover something that I could use to convince Dad to move me to Phoenix faster.

When I get home, Tūtū's tinny speakers are blasting funk on the lānai, but I don't go out to join her dance party. Instead, I survey the living room, looking for something that used to belong to Dad. I pick up the whale tail he carved for Tūtū. When I close my eyes, though, I only see the backs of my eyelids. No visions. No falling. No sudden memories.

I'm disappointed, but I suppose it makes sense. He gave that whale tail to Tūtū. It belongs to her now. Instead, I should look for something that belongs to Dad and no one else. So I head to my bedroom, where Dad's old stuff lives.

In my closet, I push aside the dresses and jackets dangling from hangers and pull out a plastic bin stuffed with Dad's favorite T-shirts. Some are stained and one even has holes in it. What do they all have in common? Dad can't get rid of them—he says they bring back memories. So, perfect! They should be what I need. I start with his high school cross-country jersey. It's got to be a memory guarantee. I close my eyes and wait . . . and wait . . . and wait.

Nothing!

That's all right, I have a whole collection of shirts to work through. Next up is a shirt for some band I've never heard of. I hold on to the fabric like my life depends on it. But after a minute I'm still sitting in my closet. I'm no closer to understanding Dad or to knowing who this band is. I go through each of Dad's shirts, gripping them and waiting, but they remain exactly what they are: old T-shirts.

Whatever memories they hold are only for Dad, not for me.

But how can these T-shirts not work if Kumu Whitman's tie did? Is it because Dad is so far away? Does the person have to be in the room with me?

I push the bin to the back of the closet again. Half-heartedly, I try holding a few other items that belonged to Dad as a kid: a baseball glove, a model airplane, a postcard from my mom. Nothing, nothing, nothing.

Out on the lānai, Tūtū has switched to a classic rock station. It's probably time to tell her I'm home before she gets worried. I don't understand what I'm doing wrong, why I can't access any of Dad's memories. As I'm about to flip off the light switch, though, I spot something Dad made. A piece of art, sort of. A doodle Dad did when he was a teenager and for some reason framed and kept all these years.

Carefully I lift the wooden frame from its hook. The glass is dusty, so I wipe it with my shirt. Then I look more closely. The drawing's not large—about half a sheet of notebook paper—but every inch is covered in pale green whorls and squiggles. Some are small, and some are large. Some are enclosed circles, and some are lines that trail off the page. On top of the squiggles are a scattering of tiny shapes—a cup, a slipper, a smiley face. They remind me of text emojis.

In the top corner is a bird, its wings outstretched, as if taking flight. Dad took the time to shade the feathers in deep black and violet pencil, so that the bird's wings seem to ripple with motion.

I've never thought to ask him about the drawing. It's always hung in the same place, small and faded and easy to forget. But now, as I hold the picture up to rehang it on its hook, something happens.

I'm seated on a fallen tree in a clearing. Nearby are saplings, each young tree bordered by fencing to protect it. It's hot out here with the sun shining down on my head and neck. Beside me, on the same downed log, are my parents. But it's not them as they are now. It's them young. High schoolers.

Mom's hair is long, all the way down to her waist. Not like now, when she keeps it short for her job. Dad is super skinny without his dad paunch. Mom puts her head on his shoulder and points to the expanse of sky in front of them. "Out there," she says. "That's where all the adventure lives." Dad takes her hand. "We've got to get off this rock," she adds.

On Dad's knees is a sketchbook, a drawing of whirls and curls.

A rustling in the bushes makes me turn my head. It's Tūtū, with her big gardening hat shading her face. Mom keeps talking about leaving the islands, all the things she and

Dad will do and see. Dad, well, that's the funny thing. I know he knows Tūtū is there, but he's pretending he doesn't.

The vision fades, I am back in my room. I've gotten what I wanted—a chance to better understand my dad, to see something that might help me move to Arizona faster. But I'm left with a sad feeling. What was Tūtū doing in this memory? And why was Dad pretending he didn't know she was there? He didn't even acknowledge Tūtū.

Maybe that's what we've been doing with Arizona, too. Failing to acknowledge her. I tease her about coming with me to Arizona, but Dad has never seriously asked her. I bet that hurts her feelings. Maybe if she knew she was welcome there, then we could all be together in Phoenix. I wouldn't even have to wait for him and Steph to get married!

I whip out my cell phone and call Dad.

"Hey, Clara. You don't usually call out of the blue. What's up?"

"I had a vision. I mean, an idea. About getting Tūtū on board with me moving to Arizona."

"Okay, shoot."

"You should invite her to move out, too. That way she would feel more involved. Like you're including her."

"I don't know . . ." Dad sounds hesitant. "She's made it pretty clear she doesn't want to leave home."

"But have you asked her? Maybe she needs to know that you'd want her in Arizona."

"You know, I never asked her to visit this summer. I feel bad about that."

"Once she's in Arizona, she'll see how happy we all are. I bet she'll want to move with me."

"Tūtū move from Hawai'i? Let's not go that far." Dad chuckles. "But if she saw how good it is for you here . . . how much happier you are . . ." He pauses. I wish I could hear what he's thinking. "You would be happier in Phoenix, right?"

"Of course! I want to go where new adventure lives."

"Funny, your mom used to say the same thing."

Twelve

TŪTŪ IS SURROUNDED BY BUCKETS. Several hold freshly harvested taro, the plants' leaves a shimmering green and the corms still dripping mud. Tūtū has already started cutting the kalo, separating the tops, the huli, for replanting from the grown corms, which we cook and eat.

"I got a jump on things," she says when I step outside. She nudges one of the buckets toward me.

I grab a huge corm, which we call the makua. "Makua" means *parent* and 'ohā are offspring or youngsters. Sure enough, this makua has two little shoots, perfect 'ohā for huli. In a few days we will press these 'ohā into the soil so they can grow and make new taro plants.

It's probably a good thing that all this kalo is in front of us for Dad's call. Tūtū will speak more gently for sure.

When her phone rings, she mumbles, "What he want today?" Then she remembers the kalo in front of her and says, louder, "Good thing it's my son."

I reach for another makua but I don't do anything with it. Just let it sit in my hand. I'm nervous for how this call is going to go.

"Hi, Mom." Dad's voice booms through the speakerphone.

"Clara's here, too," Tūtū says.

"I know."

"How you know?"

Ugh, Dad, already blowing our cover.

"She's always there with you at this time of day," he says.

Okay, good save. Can't let Tūtū think that Dad and I are working together, she'll get suspicious.

"I was thinking," Dad continues. "Would you like to visit this Christmas, with Clara? We'll go on road trips, see the Saguaro National Park. Plus, you visiting could help Clara with the eventual transition."

"Transition?"

"To living here."

Tūtū stares down at her phone as if it's an alien speaking in gibberish.

"You never got to travel when you were younger," I

92

jump in. "Dad and Mom went off adventuring, and you and Papa stayed here. Maybe it's time to get off this rock."

Tūtū looks from the phone to me and narrows her eyes. "What you say, Clara?"

"I think what Clara is trying to say," Dad intervenes, "is that this could be a good opportunity for us as a family."

"Clarence Koalani." Tūtū enunciates each syllable of my dad's name. "You not some happy-go-lucky kid anymore. You one grown man. You a father. No can be flighty, go off anywhere you like. You need for provide Clara with stability."

"Mom, I'm plenty stable."

"You need for think about roots and where you growing them. How Clara ever going for understand her place on this island? How she going continue be a part of this land, be in relationship with it, if you take her away?"

"I'm not taking her away from you. I'm offering you the chance to be with us."

"I didn't say take her away from me. I said take her away. I mean from here. From this land. From her people. Look here, Clarence. You always following some pretty wahine's idea. Why not think about what your family needs?"

"If this is about my engagement to Steph—"

"I no care about Steph—"

"That's too much, Mom. Steph has been caring toward you and Clara, and she and I love each other. She's going to be part of my life, and Clara's, whether you care or not."

"I not talking about Steph."

"But I am. You said before that our relationship was moving too fast, so I guess I should have seen this coming. But I am thinking about family and what they need, and Clara needs her dad."

"Koalani—" Tūtū tries to interrupt him.

"You know what, I've had enough of this. I've been trying to compromise, Mom, but you won't even meet me halfway. At Christmas break, I'm going to pack up Clara and bring her back to Arizona with me. You're always welcome to join us, but we're not dragging this out anymore."

I feel a thrill of excitement run from my stomach up to my throat. I'm going to get to move to Arizona! And I don't even have to wait a whole school year. Just eight weeks! But then I look at Tūtū. Her cheeks are bright red and her eyes have grown bright with tears. She bites her lip, as if fighting to keep the tears from falling, and I feel something heavy inside my heart. I want to leave here, but I don't want her to be sad when I do.

"I should have done this sooner," Dad says. "Clara's been asking to move for nearly three months now."

"That long?" Tūtū whispers to me.

I nod. "Since the first day of sixth grade."

Tūtū closes her eyes. Her expression is pained.

"I'm sorry our plan didn't work out, Clara," Dad says. "But I'm looking forward to Christmas. I love you." Then Tūtū's phone goes silent. Dad hung up.

Tūtū doesn't look at me. Instead, she looks at each of the mākua and their ʻohā spread across the patio table. "I'm sorry," she whispers. Gently, she touches the corms, the leaves, the roots. "Shrub," she says, her voice thick with emotion. "Why your dad go and say 'our plan'?"

"Because I'm the one who told him to invite you to Arizona." My voice is so small, even I can barely hear it.

"And why did you say it's time for 'get off this rock'?"

"It's something I heard Mom say once."

Tūtū lifts her gaze from the taro plants in front of her. Her eyes get big and her brows go up-up-up, and I know a new thought is dawning on her. "Clara, is there something you're not telling me?"

I shake my head, but I can't look her in the eye.

"Is there any way you went hear things you never hear before?" she prompts.

Reluctantly, slowly, I meet her gaze. "I guess you could say that."

Thirteen

TŪTŪ TELLS ME TO START from the beginning, so I begin with the morning bus ride to school. I tell her about the boys' thoughts, booming so loud I couldn't even think straight. I describe Kumu Whitman's memory. I even tell her about the fight between Denny and Brandon and how I thought I could use my power to get Brandon to stop calling me names. Finally, I tell her about this afternoon, finding Dad's drawing and seeing into his memory. I saw how sad she was hearing Dad and Mom making plans to leave, so I suggested Dad invite her to Arizona. That way she'd know she was included.

"Oh, Shrub," she says when I finish. "Back then, I not sad because I feel left out. I sad because I worry your dad go for follow a dream that's not his."

"What do you mean?"

"Your mom is one exceptional woman. I never know one wahine or kāne who at thirteen decides for become a warrant officer. But your mom knew. She had one vision for her life. Saw herself flying those Apache helicopters. And she went make it happen. She went after something. Not follow someone else's vision. Not run away like your dad."

"What was Dad running away from?"

"You not the only one can hear things, you know."

"Wait, can Dad? Can you?" Apparently, I come from a family of mind readers, and no one has ever told me. "Can you read boys' minds?!"

"No way," Tūtū says with a laugh.

I don't get why she's laughing. She just told me our family hears things. If she can't read boys' minds, then what *can* she do? "Tūtū, do you have your own superpower?"

"It's not a superpower. It's one gift. An ability to listen, for the sake of ourselves and for others." Tūtū lifts her arm to motion to the whole of our backyard. In the lo'i the leaves of the taro shimmer a deep emerald. The 'ōhi'a trees are filled with exploding red blossoms, and the 'ōhelo bushes are laden with juicy berries.

Even plants introduced to the islands are flourishing. Tūtū's plumeria produces blooms in pink, yellow, and a rare blue. Her crown flowers are tipped in magenta, the stalks reaching high above my head. Everywhere I see the results of Tūtū's love and care for her plants and respect for the soils they grow in. I understand without her having to say it.

"Papa used to say you have a green ear."

She smiles and nudges a bucket of kalo toward me. "They need a little care now."

I get the picture. If we're going to tell family stories, then we're going to mālama the family, too. Leave it to Tūtū. I'm experiencing superhuman powers that apparently she knew were coming, and she still wants to be sure we're caring for those around us. So, I pull on a pair of gloves and get to cutting 'ohā from mākua.

"It's your turn to start from the beginning," I tell her.

"Maybe you went guess, but the 'umeke can help its caretaker hear things others cannot. Its name means for listen carefully, attentively."

"Lohepono," I say. "Lohe means to listen."

"Lohe also means for obey."

"Wait, am I supposed to obey boys?"

"Not even!" Tūtū laughs. "But you do need for learn to listen responsibly."

"What does that mean?"

"Let's say I have one invasive weed that wants for get planted everywhere. I not going for do that. I need for care for the entire garden, the whole community. Or think of my brother, your uncle Kaimana."

I think of Dad going out fishing with Uncle Kai, always coming back with the most beautiful, big ulua. "What happened with Uncle Kai?"

"He can hear fish. So in our hanabata days, he helped 'em proliferate and he always had the best catch, but he not think beyond those kine fish. He not realize he no can hear mollusks, like octopus, or other kine sea creatures. Once he let the ulua eat all the he'e, no more. And then the ulua need for move to another bay. Took a long time bring the octopus back and make things right."

"But, Tūtū, boys aren't plants or fish."

"Eh, not all the listening tied to plants or animals. My tūtū, your great-great-grandmother, was gifted the ability for hear those in pain. She went get plenty schooling. Traditional kine medicine from her auntie. Nursing training from the navy. Can you imagine what she went go through during World War One? Almost like a curse sometimes. Hear folks hurting like that."

I shake my head. I cannot imagine. The ability to hear seems like a tricky thing. And overwhelming! Just the boys' voices on the bus were exhausting for me. "How do you avoid being overwhelmed by your plant mind reading?"

"I like for call it *flora*voyance. I guess you have clair*boy*ance." Tūtū laughs at her own joke. I'm glad she's cracking herself up, but where are my answers? Everything is still confusing to me. Everything in my world is still upside down!

When she sees the serious expression on my face, she calms down again. "It helps if you focus on doing something. Like right now, my hands caring for the kalo. The whispers fade away."

Whispers? These plants are whispering to Tūtū, and I'm getting boys yelling their thoughts at me.

"If I like focus on one plant, then I just breathe, smell the flowers, the stalk. Maybe I hold one leaf, as if it one hand. Relax. Think, what is this one trying for tell me? When I went working for restore that koa grove on Big Island, the whole world open up sometimes. I hold one sapling and I see it as one seed, then one full-grown tree. All the possibility."

"That sounds like what Kumu Whitman's memory did for me," I say, thinking of what happened when I held his school tie. Not exactly a world of possibility, but a better sense of Kumu Whitman.

"Okay, we all pau for now," Tūtū announces.

"Talking?"

"No, silly. With the kalo."

I look around the table and realize we've cut and sorted everything. The mākua are ready to steam; the 'ohā are ready for planting. The wide leaves are ready to be made into lū'au. And Tūtū seems calm, as if the phone call with Dad never even happened.

"Let's take some of this in and get dinner going,"

For the rest of the evening, I pepper Tūtū with questions and she answers with family stories. The time Uncle Kai got in an argument with a shark. How my great-grandmother met my great-grandfather when she was nursing him. I don't forget to ask Tūtū about my science project, either. "Bring those boys over here. You read their minds and tell me what they really think of your old tūtū," she jokes.

Later, while I finish my homework, Tūtū settles into her bed with a book. When I peek in on her later, she's sound asleep, her reading glasses askew on her nose and her book still open on her chest. Gently, I place her glasses and book on her bedstand and turn out the lights.

With Tūtū asleep, the house is quiet in a new way. When she was telling me stories and answering my questions, I felt excited about my gift. Now, by myself, I'm less sure. I'm getting to move to Arizona. That's cool. It's what I wanted. But there was a price to pay. I've never seen Dad get that mad, nor Tūtū look that hurt.

Or earlier today, with Brandon and Denny. I tried to use my powers to get something I wanted, and it really backfired. Brandon got hurt. Denny got in big trouble for throwing a punch. What if he even gets expelled? I'd feel so guilty!

Maybe I need to be a little less selfish with my gift. Fix the problems I've caused. Listen responsibly, like Tūtū said. I can even help Pua make a million more friends before I leave for Arizona.

This new plan makes me feel better. More confident. Is this how Uncle Kai felt when he realized he needed to use his gift in a different way?

Which is when a bigger question hits me, one I never got an answer to. If this is a family trait, then does Dad have a gift? And if so, why didn't Tūtū tell me about it?

Fourteen

AS I GET READY FOR school the next morning, I feel nervous. What if the boys' voices have disappeared? Maybe yesterday was all a dream, or maybe the power has left me since I misused it?

But the second I walk on the bus, I know the voices haven't gone anywhere. They rise up around me. I hear Titus narrating his book. I know which of the seventh graders forgot to put on deodorant and which fifth grader forgot to eat breakfast. When Pua waves at me, I make a dash for the open seat beside her. She's got her ʻukulele on her lap, so I nestle half of it on mine.

"How are you this morning?" She tips her head and adds, "For real."

"It's, um, a little noisy." I motion to the air around me.

"Want the window open? Will that help?" She pulls down the window for me.

The bus starts up and for a split second the wind seems to drown out the voices. But then they rush back, as if carried on the breeze. *Maybe I'll try out for basketball. . . . What was the name of that guy in that movie with the car? . . . Ooh, Waimea has waves this morning.*

"Any better?" Pua asks.

I shake my head. Then I remember Tūtū's advice. I need to focus on something. So I pull out my sketchbook and start doodling the waves at Waimea. Nothing fancy, just curves and swirls. But moving my pencil helps. The voices fade. After a few minutes, I look back up at Pua. "I needed a distraction," I tell her. "My tūtū told me it would quiet everything."

"Did you tell your tūtū about"—her voice drops to a whisper—"the voices?"

"You won't believe what she said." I fill Pua in on everything that happened last night: the 'umeke, my uncle Kai, my tūtū's own "green ear." I'm about to tell Pua about my resolution to use my gift the right way when Leo boards the bus. He's all alone. No Denny. He has his Giants cap pulled low over his face and his thoughts are a whirlwind. I can barely catch a full sentence: *Denny's mom said she'd drive only him . . . but both of them suspended from the bus . . . how I couldn't stop . . .* Leo plunks into the seat behind Pua and me.

"I think Denny and Brandon have been suspended from riding the bus," I whisper to Pua.

She motions toward her 'ukulele. "Does that mean we can take this off our laps?"

"Wait until Waialua, to make sure." Sure enough, at the Waialua stop there's no Brandon. Only Michelle. She saunters to the seat across from Pua and me before realizing that Leo is alone, looking glum.

"Want to sit with me?" Michelle asks him. "Crystal is sick today."

"That's okay." Leo goes back to peering out the window. *What if they get kicked out for good? What if they never talk to each other again? What if they never talk to me?* Leo's thoughts are filled with questions, so many there's no room for anything else.

Michelle looks crestfallen. She has no idea what's spinning in his head. When she sees me watching, her expression turns. "What's your problem, Baby Mouse?"

I look away.

"What's *her* problem?" Pua mumbles.

"She wants Leo's attention," I whisper back.

"You can read Michelle's mind now?"

"That didn't take any mind reading. Look at her." Michelle is leaning into the aisle and smiling at the back of Leo's head.

"Maybe you can convince her that the way to Leo's heart is by doing our group project at Kaluanui Stream instead of Waikīkī." Pua cracks a smile.

"Yeah, right." I chuckle. But the more I think about it, the more it seems like a good idea. I told myself I'd use my gift to help Pua.

I lean into the aisle. "Hey," I hiss at Michelle. "I know why Leo is ignoring you."

Michelle raises her eyebrows, skeptical. But then her curiosity gets the better of her. She scoots closer to me.

"Leo is really worried about his grades in Kumu Whitman's class. He doesn't want to do the group project in Waikīkī. He wants to do it at Kaluanui Stream."

"Really? I thought if we studied the Ala Wai Canal . . ." She trails off. "It doesn't matter. If that's why he's being so quiet, then we'll change the location." Michelle smooths her hair and puts on a big smile. "Hey, Leo."

He turns from his window. The questions and worries are running fast and furious, but he tries to focus on Michelle.

"We can do our group project at Kaluanui Stream if you want," she says.

"Sure, okay."

She leans forward to talk to him more, but he's back at the window. . . . *And when Denny's mom called my mom, I couldn't even explain how . . .*

Michelle is taken aback. She stutters something at Leo, stops herself. As she turns toward me, her eyes narrow. "Thanks a lot," she hisses. "I don't know why I thought you'd know anything. Leo's not friends with you anymore anyway."

Her words sting like only the truth can. I feel like I've had my breath taken from me.

Pua leans across me. "They may not be tight anymore," she says, "but Clara knows him better than anyone."

I gape at Pua. What is she doing? Trying to get Michelle even madder at us?

But Michelle bites her tongue. "Okay, then. How do I get his attention?" She folds her arms and tilts her head. I am being judged, and I know it.

I don't want to help Michelle. In fact, if Leo is too distracted to pay attention to her, that seems great to me. But Michelle is waiting to see me fail, and I want to prove her wrong. "He likes music . . . ," I start.

"Everyone likes music," she shoots back. "Tell me something I don't know."

Her voice is a demand. All this time she's either ignored me or made fun of me, and now, even when she wants something from me, she's still acting like she's doing me the favor. It makes me so mad! I want her to leave me alone. Or better yet, I want her to be embarrassed the way I was. Let everyone call her some silly name.

"Serenade him," I say, the words leaving my mouth before I've fully thought through them. But once I've said them, a plan starts forming. "Sing as loud as you can. He can't ignore you then."

"In front of everyone?" she gasps. "I couldn't do that."

"Then don't. I'm just telling you what Leo likes." My heart is pounding in my ears. Leo hates being the center of attention. If she really does this, he will be so mad at her. And everyone else will laugh.

Michelle retracts from the aisle. Everything is quiet in her seat.

"There's no way she really sings," Pua whispers to me.

Pua's right. I tried to push Michelle too far.

Then, softly at first, a voice warbles. "Somewhere over the rainbow . . ."

The bus hushes. Titus pokes his head above the seat

back. Everyone's looking around, trying to figure out who's singing.

". . . way up high." Michelle's voice is pretty. I can't deny that. And she caresses the lyrics like Iz used to.

"Oh, somewhere over the rainbow." She motions at me to join her, but I shake my head. *No way!* Pua grabs my hand. Is this really happening?

"And the dreams . . ." Michelle's lonely voice falters. Everyone's staring at her, and it's got to be embarrassing.

"That you dreamed of," a seventh grader joins in. Michelle smiles, increases the volume a little.

"Once in a lullaby." Two fifth graders add their voices.

Michelle glances at Leo, but he's still gazing out the window. It doesn't matter. The momentum is there. One by one, sixth and seventh graders add their voices. Pua drops my hand. It's unreal.

"Someday I'll wish . . . ," sings Titus. He bobs his head and smiles at me.

Next thing I know, Pua is singing along, too. "Upon a—"

"What are you doing?" I hiss at her.

"I know this one!" she says happily.

The song spreads from one row to the next, toward the back of the bus with the eighth graders and toward the front with the elementary kids. And even when I search for boys' thoughts, all I hear are lyrics.

The only two people not singing are me and Leo. He's totally lost in his thoughts. And I'm totally mystified. Is my life now a musical?

In the final lines, Titus takes the harmony, and Michelle blends her voice with his. It's gorgeous, even I have to admit that. Leo glances over and smiles, and Michelle's face lights up. He takes his baseball cap off, and for a moment it seems like she's broken through to him. But then he pulls the hat back on, tugs it even lower over his eyes than before, and looks back out the window. We're on the freeway now, speeding by exit signs.

"Oooh, ooh, oooh," she sings, and the song trails off as suddenly as it began. Kids giggle, but they're not laughing at her. They're just kind of . . . happy. They nudge each other and gently tease the ones who forgot the words or have amazing voices. Michelle hums a little more, but no one joins in. No one calls her a Singing Mouse, or whatever ridiculous nickname Denny probably would have thought up.

And I can't help but think, *This isn't fair!* Someone *else* ruins my sketchbook and I'm forever known as Baby Mouse. Michelle launches into song on the bus, and everyone joins in?

Michelle leans over to me. "Leo looked at me. But now he's back at the window."

Really? That's all she has to say? I would be terrified that I'd never live this moment down, and Michelle is only bummed Leo is in his own world?!

"Michelle," I say, exasperated, "if you need his attention so badly, then do something he can't ignore. Like this." I lean over the back of my seat and grab Leo's Giants cap off his head. Then I fling it out the open window.

For a moment, the hat catches an updraft caused by the rush of cars, and it rises. And then, whoosh. It's behind us. Leo snaps his head around to watch it land on the highway. A car runs over the brim before the whole hat is gone.

"WHO THREW THAT OUT THE BUS?" Kumu Maka's voice booms. Everyone goes silent. I'm still kneeling on the bus seat, my hand next to the open window. Quickly, I drop back down.

Kumu Maka takes the very next off-ramp. This is not an exit we ever take. "What are they doing?" someone whispers aloud.

Boys' thoughts fill the air around me. I'm sure they're no different from anybody else's.

What happened? Are we all in trouble? What went out the window? Who threw it?

Among the buzz, I hear Leo's thought, quiet and confused. *Why did Clara ruin my favorite hat?*

The bus parks on the street and Kumu Maka turns off the engine. Slowly they rise to face all of us. "Throwing things out the window is no joke. Someone—an innocent driver—could have been hurt. Whichever one of you is responsible, you gotta step forward now."

Fifteen

MY WHOLE BODY IS TREMBLING as I raise my hand. "It was me." I can hear the waver in my own voice.

"Who's that?" Kumu Maka's words echo against the bus walls.

"It's Clara," calls out some seventh grader.

"Come to the front of the bus, Clara."

I stare at the grooves in the rubber matting on the floor. I can't lift my head. I can't look anywhere except at the floor. I can't even look at Pua. I'm so embarrassed and ashamed. I've never gotten in trouble like this. I've never done something like this!

I don't know what I was thinking. I'd just had *enough*.

I can feel the tears threatening but I don't want to cry

in front of everyone. Not again. Not like at the beginning of the year.

Somehow I make it down the long bus aisle and come to a stop in front of Kumu Maka. I can't look at them either. Only the tips of their black boots.

"Clara, I'm surprised it's you," they murmur.

"I—I—I—" The tears are spilling over my cheeks, but no one can see them. No one except Kumu Maka. If I don't talk, maybe the tears will stop.

"Sit in the seat across from me. Where I can see you." Their voice is soft but firm. I nod and sit. Louder and with total command, Kumu Maka announces, "Listen up, everyone. Never throw anything out the window. Not only is it against the law, it's really dangerous. If a car swerved or the item hit their windshield, it could cause an accident. You got me?"

A few kids murmur their assent.

"Let's try again. You got me?"

"Yes, Kumu Maka," the whole bus says back.

"Good." They turn to me and, quiet again, say, "Don't leave with everyone else when we get to school, 'kay? I need for report this."

I force myself to look up. I expect Kumu Maka to appear really angry, but they actually just look shaken. I feel even worse than before. It's their job to keep all of us safe, and I messed with that.

For the rest of the bus ride, I let the voices wash over me. I can't focus on anything enough to keep them at bay. Elementary school kids are talking about how I nearly caused a car accident. Some little boy is thinking about a fender bender his mom was in, and remembering it makes him scared all over again. I feel terrible. And that's not the only thing. The older kids, the ones who know me, are all wondering *why* I threw Leo's hat.

Does Clara hate the Giants? Are Michelle and Clara fighting over Leo? Was Clara trying to impress the new girl? Does Clara have any friends anymore? I sink lower in the seat and wipe my face.

Beside me, a Hawaiian shirt wrapped in a plastic dry-cleaning bag is laid out with care. It must be Kumu Maka's. I look at it and only it. I don't want to look out the window, where all those cars are—cars that could have been in an accident because of my carelessness. I don't want to look up, for fear of catching Kumu Maka's eye. And I definitely don't want to look behind me, at the whole bus. So I stare at the shirt, its alternating pattern of white and yellow. It's the one thing that's safe.

When we get to school, I have to stay seated while

everyone streams past me. It's not so bad when it's the younger kids. But when it's my grade, it's humiliating. I shrink away from the aisle. Titus stares at me as he passes. *What is going on with Clara?* Michelle looks worried, which I suppose is kind of nice coming from her. Leo ignores me, but I know what's running through his mind. *How could Clara do that? She knows what that hat means to me. Does she hate me?*

I don't hate you, I want to answer him.

Only Pua pauses. "What was that?" she whispers as she hands me my backpack. But then she's gone, too.

When the bus has emptied, Kumu Maka radios the main office to let them know what I did. Kumu Apo radios back that she'll come down to escort me. With that settled, Kumu Maka turns in their seat to face me. "You want tell me why you went throw that hat out the window?" Their voice is calm.

I open my mouth to explain. How Leo was distracted. How Michelle wanted his attention. How I felt so angry at her for being mean to me all these weeks until today, when she wanted me to help her communicate with Leo. All of it.

But I end up closing my mouth again. A sob is stuck in my throat. I twist at a corner of the plastic dry-cleaning bag. It helps me hold back the tears. "I just wanted Leo's attention," I manage finally.

"You two used to be besties, yeah?" Kumu Maka asks.

I nod. Grab a little more of the plastic bag.

"Hard when friendships shift."

I nod again. A corner of Kumu Maka's shirt catches in my hand, and I cling to it. The fabric is silky, comforting. Like a lifeline of some sort. I squeeze.

"Ē, Clara! That's my best shirt."

Oh no! I've left creases everywhere! "I'm sorry!" I smooth out the shirt as best I can.

"You're something today!" Kumu Maka rests their hand on my head for a moment and then asks, "What do you see in this fabric?"

"Wrinkles?"

"Other than that," they urge. "What's the pattern?"

I study it. Sleek white silhouettes repeating themselves against a yellow background. Slender beaks, outspread wings. "Birds?"

They pick up the shirt and shake it gently. The wings undulate, as if they're flapping. "'Iwa," they say.

I gasp. "My tūtū told me about those. Aren't they thieves?"

"That's one story about 'iwa. I have my own." They hand back the shirt. "Go ahead, take the bottom."

I run my fingers across the silky fabric, careful not to wrinkle it again.

"Now," they say, "look at those mountains out there." I peer through the bus window at the Waiʻanae Mountain Range, brown and hazy in the distance. They are different from my lush green Koʻolaus.

"What do you see?" Kumu Maka asks.

"Brown?"

"Try again," they instruct patiently. "Close your eyes."

I close my eyes . . . and after a moment, I am falling!

I stumble, find myself clinging to a tree trunk. Beneath me, the earth is uneven with roots and rocks. I try to get my bearings, but I cannot see beyond my own hands, my own feet. It's like being underwater without goggles. Everything is blurred.

Nearby is a shuffling noise. Someone runs in one direction, then another. Light footfalls. A keiki, like me. Not an adult.

This vision is unlike the ones with Kumu Whitman and Dad. There I saw everything, and I knew what they were thinking and feeling. Here, I am not in charge.

"Hey," I call out. "Who's there?" I am afraid to let go of the tree, afraid I will lose all sense of my bearings.

The footsteps come close again. A hand clasps mine and pulls me forward.

And then, it's as if I've emerged from being underwater. Suddenly my vision is clearer, sounds are crisper. I look at my arm, my hand, the hand holding mine, another slender arm. I follow until I am gazing at my companion. I recognize immediately the big brown eyes, the 'ūpepe nose. "Is that you, Kumu Maka?" I ask. "Can you see me?"

"I see you, Clara." The keiki smiles at me, but it's Kumu Maka's grown-up voice I hear.

"How are you talking to me?"

"I went guess your power. I have some of my own, too. Come, I want for show you this memory."

We spin slowly around, the keiki and me.

"Many years ago, when I was your age, I got lost in these mountains." We're surrounded by trees, and they all look the same. No trail. No way to distinguish one direction from another. We can't even rely on the sky—a canopy of branches and leaves block the sunlight. But then, up ahead, we notice a bright spot, a break in the canopy. We run toward it.

In that small opening, the sky is cloudless, so pale blue it's almost white. Which direction do we go from here? Beside me, I hear soft chanting, but the 'ōlelo comes too fast for me to comprehend. A shadow crosses overhead. A bird, circling. I feel a chill. In movies buzzards always appear when someone is lost in the desert and going to die. Should I be afraid?

119

Kumu Maka's voice interrupts my thoughts. "I asked Kaiona, Goddess of Ka'ala, for help, and she sent an 'iwa to guide me to safety."

The 'iwa catches a current of air and stops its circling, kiting instead. With its wings outspread, it's like a giant arrow, pointing in one direction. That's where we need to go.

As the memory disappears, I open my eyes. I'm clutching the 'iwa shirt, not someone's hand. Kumu Maka is sitting next to me on the bus seat.

"How'd you do that?" I ask. "You knew I was there."

"What you can see is limited," they say. "I helped expand it."

I feel my eyes widen. I'm amazed. "But Kumu, what gift do you have?"

"Gift?"

"That's what my tūtū calls my, um, power."

"Gift, mmm. I like that." Gently, Kumu Maka takes the shirt from me and drapes it over the seat next to ours. "Hard, sometimes, find your place, especially when you have a gift. Can make mistakes along the way, can hurt others or yourself even."

"I didn't want to hurt Leo. I'm really sorry about his hat."

"I know you're sorry. But next time you like get one

boy's attention, act nice. Compliment the hat. Don't go throw it out a window. Okay?"

"Okay." I duck my head in embarrassment.

Kumu Maka points me back to the mountains. "That 'iwa you saw. It didn't just get me to a trail. It led me right into another hiking group. Ends up, they the ones I really looking for. One community. Folks for teach me, understand me, guide me."

"They teach you about your gift?"

"Yes, and they help me discover another."

"Really?" Kumu Maka is full of surprises.

"I have one magic kine gift, like yours. Mines lets me see memories and share them. But I have another kine gift that comes from a lifetime of building a place in the middle, being māhū. I can see things from more than one perspective. So I can see that you're lost, but I can also see that, with a little more direction, you can find yourself."

"Are you going to give me that direction?"

"I'm no 'iwa!" Kumu Maka laughs. "Up to you decide what direction you like take. And up to you for pay attention to who gonna help you get there."

My head is spinning. Kumu Maka is like Tūtū. They speak clearly, yet I'm not always sure what they mean. Out the window, I see Kumu Apo walking across the field to come get me. I have so many questions left for Kumu Maka, but I have time for only one.

"Why'd you bring your 'iwa shirt today? Was it for me?"

"Not everything about you, Clara." They tease. "I actually wear this shirt anytime I'm nervous. It reminds me I'm never alone."

"Why are you nervous?"

"I'm having my photograph taken this afternoon for an interview with the paper. My artwork has been chosen for the Honolulu Biennial. This big art exhibition."

"Wow, Kumu. Are you famous?"

"I wish!" They laugh again. "But it feels good to be recognized for something I love. Something I've been working at for a long time. So, I get nervous but I'm grateful, too."

"That's really cool." I want to hear more, but Kumu Apo is rapping on the open door of the bus.

"I'm here to take Clara up to the office."

Just when I was feeling better, my face flushes again and my body starts to tremble.

"Go easy on Clara," Kumu Maka says. "She made a mistake, but she understands what she did wrong, and she's apologized. She definitely won't be doing this again."

"I have to admit, I was surprised when I heard it was

Clara," Kumu Apo says. She turns to me. "Let's head up to the office."

I nod and follow her down the stairs. Just before we leave, though, I turn back to Kumu Maka. "Good luck this afternoon! Can't wait to see your picture in the paper!"

Sixteen

KUMU APO'S OFFICE IS A small room set behind the attendance desk. Two tall filing cabinets guard the door, but what impresses me the most is all the shelves. They line three sides of the room, and every single one is filled with books.

"Whoa," I say, looking around. "Did you read all these?"

"I did." Kumu Apo chuckles. "You want the tour?"

"There's a tour?"

"The books on this wall are all about education. They help me think about how I want to teach and mentor and discipline." She pauses to give me a look. I get it, the discipline is coming soon enough. "The ones back there are children's and young adult books. Fiction, nonfiction, novels and poetry, comics and graphic novels. Anything that I think you folks might enjoy."

"Isn't the library for that?"

"The library is for students to read them. But I keep my own copies. So I can talk books with you."

I point to the wall to her left. "And what are those?"

"All these here, this whole wall, is filled with literature from Hawai'i and the Oceanic region, by authors from across the Pacific Ocean."

"But this is the biggest wall."

"And Oceania is the biggest region in the world. We're part of that. We've got big stories."

After this morning with Leo's hat, I feel like shrinking into a ball. "I think I'm someone with a small story."

"Maybe, all alone, your story is on the small side. Most stories, taken by themselves, can feel that way. Like how an island that stands alone in a huge sea can look small. But if you stop looking at that one island and instead see how it's part of a whole archipelago, how the Pacific is filled with islands, then you might start to notice how big your story actually is. How much space and time and how many connections it covers."

I don't even know how to reply. Kumu Apo's words, like Kumu Maka's, make me think I have to look at everything in a different way.

Kumu Apo motions to the chair in front of her desk and

I sit down. "We might also think about the connections we have with other people," she says. "You're not an island, or a story, unto yourself. Your actions have repercussions."

I hang my head. "I know." I had almost forgotten why I was here, but now the shame and nerves are back.

"Maka said you apologized to them, and that means a lot. But we still have to address the fact that you threw something out the window. And that I'm sure Leo is disappointed to have had his hat taken and lost."

"It's one of his favorites, too," I mumble.

Kumu Apo lets out a long sigh that makes me a little anxious. She stares at her bookshelves, right and left, and the one on the far wall behind me. "I've got an idea," she says. "Next week you'll do school service at lunch. Restocking books in our library."

A week ago, I would have jumped at the chance to have a lunchtime activity. Now I feel disappointed. Just when I've found someone to eat lunch with, I'll be hanging out with a bunch of books instead.

"One more thing," Kumu Apo says. "I want you to write apology notes to both Kumu Maka and Leo. You can do it before you head to first period."

I grimace.

"Is there a problem?"

"No, no," I say. Writing to Kumu Maka is fine. Talking to them this morning helped, so I know what I want to say. The note to Leo is different. I don't even know where to start. "I can write Kumu Maka's note right away. But I need more time with Leo's."

"That's fair. Write Kumu Maka's now, before the homeroom bell rings. You can show me Leo's at the end of the day. Does that work?"

"That works. Thank you."

"You're welcome." Kumu Apo smiles at me. "Now scoot. I've got another meeting, and it's not going to be as easy as yours."

I let myself out of Kumu Apo's office. There's an empty corner beside the attendance desk where I can write my letters. I pull out my notebook and start: *Dear Kumu Maka.*

Just then the door from the main hall opens and in walks Denny. When he sees me, he saunters over. "Hey," he says, all casual.

"What are you doing here?"

"Relaxing." He crosses his arms and leans against the wall. *This is a stupid idea for a stupid meeting. I don't care what Kumu Apo says.*

So *that* is Kumu Apo's next meeting! No wonder she said it wasn't going to be easy.

"Why are *you* here?" he asks.

"Didn't you hear about the bus?"

He shakes his head. *The one day I don't ride the bus and something big happens.*

"I kind of got in trouble. Threw Leo's hat out the window."

"Ohhhhh shoot!" *Clara never gets in trouble! I gotta tell Brandon about— No, I don't have to tell Brandon anything. He doesn't deserve to know.* "Why'd you do that?"

"I was trying to help Michelle get Leo's attention. Not that she needs my help."

"She definitely needs your help." *Michelle's been crushing on Leo for so long.*

"Wait, Michelle likes Leo? Like, like-likes?"

"Oh, you know about that?" *I thought she only told me and Crystal. But whatever.* "Leo is totally oblivious. You probably know that, too."

I DON'T KNOW ANY OF THIS! I want to scream.

"You being Leo's best friend and all."

"I'm not his best friend anymore. I thought maybe you were."

"I'm Brandon's best friend. I mean, I was. We're not best friends anymore either." *I don't know how Brandon and I were ever friends. When we get in with Kumu Apo, I'm going*

to tell him he has to return all the stuff I've let him borrow.
And the three dollars he owes me for lunch last week. And—

"How long has Michelle liked Leo?"

"Why you asking?" *Did I spill something?*

"Oh, you know." I've got to be as casual as Denny if he's going to tell me anything. If he's even going to *think* anything. So I cross my arms like him, and I lean toward the wall. But it's farther away than I realize. I feel myself tipping and I can't stop. I slide onto the floor in a heap.

"Are you okay?"

I wait for Denny to laugh, but instead he holds out a hand to help me back up.

"I meant to do that." I brush away Denny's hand and stand up on my own.

"Are you sure? You've been different the last few days."

"Different? What do you mean?" Oh no! Could Denny have figured out what's going on? I wait to hear his thoughts but, for once, there's nothing. He's waiting for me. Waiting for what I'm going to tell him.

Part of me wants to run out of the office, forget about apology notes and class. Anything to avoid telling Denny the truth. Part of me wants to lie, tell Denny I'm great and falling on the floor is one of hobbies. But part of me—the smallest part—also wants to do something I never believed possible: trust him. "These last couple of days have been hard," I confess. "I'm moving to Arizona."

"Whoa! 'Cause of your dad?"

I nod.

"When do you leave?"

"Over Christmas break."

"I guess you must be happy?"

"I guess."

"It's not going to be the same around here without you." I wait to hear some sarcastic thought from Denny, but instead I get something else. Not a thought really. More a feeling. A tinge of sadness.

"I doubt you'll miss me," I say, to keep things light.

"I will." He's serious. Not playing around. "You're funny and smart and you bring out the best in people. I'm not crushing or anything. I'm just stating facts."

I'm stunned into silence. I didn't know Denny thought of me in such a nice way. I didn't know he thought about me at all. "If you thought all this, why didn't you ever say hi? Or sit next to me on the bus? Or whatever."

Denny shrugs. "I dunno. Seems like this year you've wanted space. You kind of put out the vibe that you were done with everyone here. Maybe 'cause you knew you were going to Arizona."

"That's not it." My world is reeling. All this time I assumed no one wanted to be friends with me after the Milky Mouse incident. And now, here's Denny telling me that he thought I didn't want to be friends with him, or anyone else for that matter.

Before I can say anything else, though, Brandon walks into the office. He glances at us, then looks away and heads straight for Kumu Apo's door. *Is Clara on Denny's side, too? He's the one who punched me!*

Kumu Apo invites Brandon to come inside. "I'll come back in one minute," she says to Denny.

Next to me, Denny's thoughts are working overtime. *Why does he get to go in first? What's he going to tell her? I bet Kumu Apo tries to make me apologize to Brandon.*

"What's so bad about apologizing?" I ask, before realizing I'm jumping in on his thoughts.

Thankfully, he's too worked up to notice. "Brandon's the one who started it! He should apologize to me." *Why doesn't anyone believe me? I'm not taking the blame for this fight. I shouldn't be the one who gets suspended or . . . kicked out.*

Hearing Denny's thought makes me feel really guilty. Getting expelled is serious. It could change Denny's whole life! If anyone is to blame, it's me. I'm the one who egged the two of them on with my mind reading. "I don't think you're to blame."

"Thanks, Clara. It's like you can read my thoughts this morning."

"HA HA HA." My fake laugh is so loud it startles the aunties at the attendance desk.

"Shhhh," one of them says.

Kumu Apo pops her head out of her office. "Denny, I'm ready for you now. And Clara, you can show me your letters this afternoon. This may take a while."

I glance at Denny. I don't need to hear Denny's thoughts to know what he's feeling. A look of dread is all over his face! "Good luck in there," I whisper. And then, I don't know why, I pat Denny on the shoulder. He doesn't say anything, but as he heads into the office, I hear him think, *At least Clara has my back.*

Denny's thought brings back the stone in my gut. That feeling of guilt and shame. If I really had Denny's back, he and Brandon wouldn't have gotten into their fight in the first place. If I had used my gift in a better way this morning, I could've talked to Leo about his own feelings about the fight, instead of trying to mess with Michelle.

As I walk back to class, I think about what Kumu Maka said, how one of their gifts comes from building a place in the middle. From being able to see more than one way of being, and from making a community. I look at the beautiful mural painted on the hallway walls. An ocean teeming with sea life, from tiny coral polyps to massive whales to birds skimming the surface of the waves. All living together, living in harmony, and I remember how Uncle Kai had to mend what he broke to bring back balance—not just to the bay but to his family's lives. I need to do the same. And I need to do it fast, before I move to Arizona.

So I make a vow. I will put things right between Brandon and Denny. I will make Leo see that the whole hat thing was an accident. By the time I leave this island, I will fix all my mistakes and everyone around me will be happy.

Then, maybe, I'll finally have the hang of this whole clairboyance thing.

Seventeen

AT LUNCH, PUA STEERS ME away from our bench and toward the table where Titus, Ollie, and their friend Nalu are eating. "Um, what are we doing?" I whisper. But Pua doesn't answer me. Just plops herself down, then pulls me to sit beside her.

"What's up?" Pua says to the boys, as if it's totally normal for us to be sitting with them.

"What are you doing here?" Nalu asks. He's paused in the middle of unpacking his lunch, his hands hovering in the air. He glares at Pua.

"Good question." I look pointedly at her, but Pua doesn't seem to notice our reactions, and neither does Titus.

"You said you'd convince me," Titus says, "so let's hear it."

I look from Titus to Pua and back again.

Nalu is as lost as I am. *What's going on? Why are these girls sitting with us? And what is Pua supposed to convince Titus of?*

"Three reasons to live in Narnia over Middle-earth," Pua says.

Whaaat? I thought Pua and I were going to eat together like yesterday. Just the two of us. We'd talk about the bus ride, or my gift, or literally anything other than Narnia. I look over at Nalu, thinking that at least he will feel as annoyed as I do, but he's pulling out his book and waving it around with passion. "You're totally forgetting about the elves!"

Ollie leans over to me. "Bao?"

Is that a creature I'm supposed to know? An animal noise? This lunch period keeps getting weirder.

Clara is making a face, Ollie thinks. *Is my lunch gross to her? Does no one else's family call dumplings bao?*

"Dumplings!" That makes a lot more sense. "I got confused by all the elven talk," I assure Ollie. "I love bao. What kind are these?"

"Char siu." He nudges his lunch box toward me, and I select one of the pale spheres nestled in there.

"Thanks." I take a bite, and it's the softest dough I've ever tasted. Even cold it's pillowy and yeasty and a little bit sweet. The pork inside tastes like fresh barbecue smoke and spices. "Whoa, this is amazing. Where'd you get these?"

"I made them. I like cooking."

"I've never tasted anything better. Seriously."

Ollie smiles shyly. *Maybe if Clara likes them, Hoku would like one?* He glances at a picnic table near the cafeteria.

Hoku is in my Hawaiian language class, and though I'm sure she only knows me as that girl Michelle calls Baby Mouse, she's always really nice. Plus, she can talk to anyone—in English or ʻōlelo Hawaiʻi. If Ollie has a crush on her, I understand why.

He glances at her picnic table again. *I can't walk over there with this bao in my hand. . . .*

I've vowed to mend the relationships in my life, but maybe I should think beyond myself. Help with Ollie's life, too. Plus, this could be a warm-up for my clairboyance. A test run. If I can get Ollie to talk to Hoku—and how hard can that be?—then I'll be ready to tackle the tougher stuff, like getting Denny and Brandon to talk. Or Leo and me.

I point to the dumplings in Ollie's lunch box. "Can I have another to share with a friend?"

He glances at Pua, deep in conversation with Titus and Nalu. *I doubt she wants to be interrupted for this.* "If you think so. . . ."

Oh, Ollie, if only you knew who I'm giving this to! I

pull out a napkin from my own lunch bag and carefully lay the bao in the center of it, making a neat bundle. As I head toward Hoku's table, I can hear Ollie: *Wait, what is Clara doing? Where is she going?*

Don't worry, Ollie, I want to tell him. *I've got this.*

"Hi, Hoku," I say when I reach her table. She and her best friend, Jade, look at me expectantly. "I take 'ōlelo with you," I add awkwardly.

"I know." Hoku smiles at me. "We did win the dialogue competition last month. Aloha hou mai kāua e Clara."

"Aloha kākou. Pehea 'olua?"

"Maika'i nō, mahalo," Hoku says.

"I don't how you can go back and forth," Jade moans. "Conversing like that makes me so nervous."

"We were only saying hi, how are you," I explain.

"Jade has 'ōlelo anxiety," Hoku says. "Even when it's easy, she freaks out and can't respond."

"For real?" I turn to Jade, and she nods gravely. I can't believe that Jade would be nervous about anything. She's a soloist in orchestra. She's already on a club volleyball team and has had her picture featured in the newspaper. Plus, she leaped ahead in math and is taking pre-algebra this year. Next to Jade, I feel basic. If it weren't for Ollie, I would never have approached her and Hoku. Speaking of which . . . "Ollie made these bao and they're really good. I thought you might like to try one." I set the napkin bundle on the table between Hoku and Jade.

Hoku takes a bite. "OMG, this is amazing."

"Right?" I agree. "So I have a secret for you. Ollie wants to ask someone out."

Hoku bows her head shyly, but she can't hold back her smile. "Really?"

"Maybe for a date next weekend?"

"Oh, a date?" Hoku says. "I'm not old enough to date."

"You could bring along some friends," I suggest. "Like Jade and Nalu or someone."

"That would work."

"I don't know—" Jade stretches her long legs out under the picnic table.

"Come on," Hoku begs. "It'll be fun."

Jade makes a whining noise and slumps her shoulders.

"She's being silly," Hoku says. "It's because she's so much taller than every guy in our grade. They tease her."

Tease? Jade? All I ever see is boys asking her to be on their team in PE or hang out. And she knows how to talk to them, to make them laugh. I wish I had her ease.

"They're just jealous because you dominate on the court," I tell her. "Nalu won't be like that. He's really nice."

"You sure?"

"Positive."

Jade throws her hands up in the air. "Ugh, okay, I'll go. But if anyone asks what the weather is like up here, I'm leaving."

"Thank you, thank you." Hoku hugs Jade. "Tell Ollie we'll hang out with him and Nalu."

I wave at them as I depart, all smiles. Back at our lunch table, Ollie is pretending to be absorbed in Nalu, Titus, and Pua's conversation. But I know he's not really listening to them. *What did Clara talk about with Hoku? Did she like the bao? What happened over there?!*

"You're not going to believe this," I say to Ollie, "but Hoku wants to hang out next weekend."

"Really?" I can feel Ollie's heart soaring. "Should I, like, plan a trip to the beach or maybe go-karting? That's expensive, but if a bunch of people could go . . ."

"I actually told Hoku you would bring just one friend. You and her, and Jade and Nalu."

Nalu looks at me like I'm talking gibberish. "I can't go."

"What do you mean you can't go?" Hold up! I've made a foolproof plan. There's no way Nalu can be busy all weekend.

"My family's going to Maui for a family reunion. I leave

139

next Friday after lunch. Don't get back until late Sunday night."

"But . . . but . . . ," I sputter. I can't believe this! If Nalu can't go, how do I help Ollie? This is supposed to be an easy test run for my clairboyance. If I can't accomplish this task, then what?

I need to stay calm and think. Take a deep breath, count to five. I can fix this if I try hard enough. There must be someone other than Nalu who can . . . "Titus, why don't you go? Jade is super cool."

"This isn't for me," Titus says.

"Is it because Jade is so tall? Because that's really unfair."

"No, Jade is great. That's not it at all."

"I don't love the idea of a date-date either," Ollie interrupts. His thoughts are beginning to spin out with anxiety. *I can't be one-on-one with Hoku. I'll freak out and get all silent and probably end up staring at her which is totally weird and then she'll think I'm weird and she'll never want to hang out again and—*

"Jade and I don't have much in common," Titus says. *What would we talk about? It's not like with—*

"It's just hanging out, Titus. You'll have two other people to talk to." Argh, I slipped up and answered Titus's thoughts! It's hard to keep track through all the noise of who's saying what and who's thinking it.

"Clara," Pua says softly.

"This is for your best friend, Titus," I add.

I mean, for Ollie I'd do a lot, but—

"Clara," Pua says, a little louder. "I don't think Titus—"

"If Titus is really charming, Jade may even fall for him. And wouldn't that be cute?"

"CLARA!" Pua barks at me.

"What?" I snap back, exasperated. "Don't you want everyone to be happy?"

"Don't you . . . Don't you . . ." Pua's face turns red. What is happening? "Don't you ever listen?!" Pua grabs her backpack and runs from the table. I look from Ollie to Titus and back to Ollie, but neither of them is pleased with me either.

Finally, Nalu says the thing that everyone is thinking: "Wow, Clara, you really messed that up."

Eighteen

BECAUSE IT'S FRIDAY, I HAVE study hall with Kumu Whitman for my final period. In study hall Kumu Whitman lets us sit wherever we like, and if we want to work on homework from other classes, he's fine with that.

Even though study hall is the same people as science class, the vibe is totally different. Titus and Denny sit together and start laying out what has to get done on our group project. Denny is surprisingly on top of things. He even printed out maps of the Pūpūkea area. "Lunchtime detention with Kumu Whitman paid off," I overhear him tell Titus.

Michelle says a shy hello to Leo and then asks Kumu Whitman's permission to sit with a couple of kids in her advanced ʻōlelo class. Apparently, word of Michelle's performance on the bus has gotten around, and now they want her to help with an original mele they're composing.

That means Pua and Leo are working together. But does either invite me to join them? Do either even look my way? Not at all. It's like the beginning of sixth grade all over again. Except not only have I lost Leo as a friend, I've lost Pua, too.

I don't understand how things went so wrong at lunch! Ollie wanted to talk to Hoku. Hoku likes talking to everyone. How did it end up with no one talking to *me*? And if I couldn't get that right, then how am I going to fix the bigger problems in my life? It's not just Denny and Brandon. Or Leo and me. There's Tūtū and Dad, too. When I leave for Arizona, will everyone still be mad at each other—and at me?

I rip a sheet of paper out of my notebook. The least I can do is write this apology letter to Leo. Thankfully, I managed to finish the one for Kumu Maka. But Leo's needs to be done by the end of study hall. I uncap my pen, bend over the paper, and—

TAP-TAP-TAP!

What is that?! Who is tapping me? I spin around to see Denny leaning over his desk, his hand poised in the air above my shoulder. "Hey," he says, smiling.

"Hey what?" Part of me wants to tell him to leave me alone, but he may be the only person in the world still speaking to me.

"You going to help Titus and me?"

"I have to finish this thing for Kumu Apo before the end of the period. Can you leave some task for me as homework? I'll get it done tonight."

"Sure, no prob."

"Thanks." I return to my notebook paper, take a deep breath, and refocus. I want to tell Leo I'm sorry for what I did to his hat. And that I don't hate him. And that I'd like to be friends again, but also that I don't understand why we're not friends anymore in the first place. Why did he turn his back on me at the beginning of the year?

Leo and Pua are laughing about something. When I try to listen for his thoughts, all I hear are snippets: *in the waterway . . . if we look at it a hundred years ago . . . strangers . . . like Clara said . . .*

The sound of my name makes me sit up, and I lose my focus completely. A classroom's worth of boys' voices rush in: *thirty-six minutes left of study hall . . . then we'll go biking with my brother . . . my mom won't let me skip Japanese school for even one Saturday . . . thirty-four minutes left of study hall . . .*

What was Leo thinking about me? What does he think I said? And what did he mean by strangers?

TAP-TAP-TAP!

What is it this time?

Denny is waiting for me with one of his big grins. "You want to be in charge of drawing animals or maps?"

"I don't know how to draw a map," I say, exasperated.

"Okay, then animals." Denny is as chipper as ever. He turns back to Titus.

I'm left totally disoriented. Leo, voices, Denny. Did I say Leo and I were strangers? I don't remember ever doing that. Now that's one more question for my letter. *Dear Stranger*, I write. Argh! That's not what I meant! I ball up the paper and tear out a new sheet. *Dear Leo*, I try again.

"One more thing." Denny's voice interrupts for the millionth time. Is he for real? "Titus and I are still good to go to your house tomorrow, right?"

"Yes," I say, without turning around. Maybe if I keep staring at my letter he'll get the hint.

"Can your tūtū call my mom tonight and tell her? I'm technically grounded because of the fight, but the exception is schoolwork."

"I'll tell Tūtū to call." I wave my hand over my shoulder, trying to shoo him away.

145

But now it's Titus's turn to interrupt. He actually gets up from his seat and comes to stand in front of me. "You can't forget, Clara. It's make-or-break on our project."

Ugh, it's no use ignoring them. I meet Titus's gaze. "I won't forget, okay?"

"You got my number?" Denny asks.

"You got his number?" Titus repeats.

"It's the same as last year, right?"

"Yeah."

"Then I got it."

"Got it, good." Titus taps my desk twice. What's with all this tapping? At least Titus goes back to his seat and leaves me alone. Finally, I can turn back to the paper in front of me.

It's hard to know what to say. Do I start with a greeting? *How are you today?* Leo would probably reply, *Not great, thanks to you.* Or maybe I try to explain to him what I meant to have happen? *I only wanted to get your attention for Michelle.* No, that's too much of an excuse. Or I simply dive in? *I'm sorry that I—*

TAP-TAP-TAP!

This time Denny is poking at both shoulders!

"What?!" I snap. I spin around so fast, I lose the grip on my pencil. It flies across the aisle, nearly stabbing Titus in the leg. He jumps.

"Sheesh, Clara," Denny says. "Dramatic much? My question can wait."

"You've got my attention now."

"Well, I wanted to know if you like to hike."

"Huh?" How is this at all important? I drop to the floor and go crawling after my pencil. Titus and Denny just watch. Really, guys? When I find my pencil, I try to stand up—only to hit my head on Titus's desk. "Ouch!" I yelp.

"That looks like it hurt," Titus says sympathetically. "You've got to pay attention to where your head's at."

I'd love to, Titus! I want to scream. *If you guys would let me!* I collapse back into my chair. Denny is still leaning over his desk and smiling at me. What is it now?

"Are the trails near your house any good? Should we go hiking after our project is done?"

"Um, maybe?" I say. Denny waits for more. I feel a little bad for being so frustrated with him and Titus. They're actually being really nice, and Denny is trying to include me. "The trails above my house are in the forest. I don't remember if there are any lookouts. I haven't been up there for a while. Not since my dad moved. Anyway, I prefer hikes by the ocean."

"Cool," Denny says. *Cool,* Denny thinks. He turns to Titus. "What's your favorite hike by the ocean?"

"Makapuʻu has good views."

"Too easy. Pill Boxes is better."

My words echo in the air around me. . . . *Hikes by the ocean . . . hikes by the ocean . . .*

I'm glad for the sake of our group project that Denny and Titus are getting along so well, but I'm also confused. Is that all it takes for them to suddenly be best buds? A conversation about hiking? Honestly, reading boys' minds does not help me understand them any more than I did before. I'm as lost as ever!

. . . eighteen minutes left of study hall . . .

And as behind as ever! I have to get this letter done before I see Kumu Apo. *Dear Leo*, I repeat to myself. Then I write: *I'm sorry for what I did on the bus this morning.*

"Kaʻena." Leo's voice distracts me. He's got his elbow on Denny's desk. "You're forgetting Kaʻena Point. That's my favorite."

"That's a great one," Denny agrees. Titus nods.

I close my eyes and listen for something more from Leo. . . . *Over the sand dunes . . . where my dad and I would go fish . . . on Sunday when Mom and I—*

Twelve minutes left of study hall! Someone else's thought interrupts Leo's. I glare at the boy in front of me. Stop counting down minutes, Rizal!

148

But Leo's thoughts are gone again, lost in the mix, and no matter how hard I try I can't pick them out. It's all word salad. I give up. I put away my notebook, zip my backpack shut.

"Can I go to the Po'o Kumu's office?" I ask Kumu Whitman.

"Better hurry," he says, handing me a hall pass.

At least the halls are quiet. Still, I feel overwhelmed. Lost. I tried really hard to use my gift the right way today. Even so, I messed everything up.

As I cross from the science wing to the admin building, I pause. There's this beautiful view of the Wai'anae Mountains. In the afternoon haze, their silhouette is blue gray against the bright blue sky.

I think of the 'iwa that hovered over me in the Foodland parking lot on the same day I made my request of the 'umeke. Could it have been sent to guide me, like Kaiona sent the 'iwa to guide Kumu Maka? Because I could really use more direction. The way things are going, my gift is turning out to be a curse.

Nineteen

ON THE BUS RIDE HOME, I sit alone. Though Kumu Apo has approved my apology letters, I don't dare give Leo his. He's sitting with Michelle. She'd probably read it aloud to the whole bus. Across from me, Pua and Titus share a seat, and Titus actually chats the entire ride, not once pulling out his book. I wish I could join them, but I'm afraid if I try, Pua will tell me to go away, so I stay gazing out the window, watching the Waiʻanae Mountains in the distance.

When I get home, I look for Tūtū. All I want is to give her a big hug, feel her wrap me in her strong arms. So I'm surprised when I find her in her bedroom, lying down with the lights off. "No worry about me," she says when I open the door wide. "Just a little tired this afternoon." When she inhales, a whistling noise tells me her asthma is acting up.

I kiss her gently on the cheek. "You want me let you rest?"

"No, no. I be up in one minute."

"No rush, Tūtū. I can cook if you want."

"Mmmm. That might be good, Shrub." Tūtū rolls over in her bed. In the cool, dim light her back is as shadowed as the mountainside. "Close the door behind you, yeah." I close the door, and in the silence of the hallway feel deeply alone. No Pua to text, no Tūtū to talk to.

So I call Mom.

She picks up on the third ring. "Hey, baby," she says. I wince at being called "baby." Sometimes she forgets that I don't like that word since everything that went down at the start of the year.

"What are you doing?" I ask. Mom is based in Alaska these days. Last week she texted me pictures of the first frost. I texted back a photo of Waimea Bay, the water glassy and inviting.

"I finished up dinner and now I'm going to feed Togo." Togo is Mom's husky, named after a famous Alaskan sled dog. "You want to say hi?"

"Hi, Togo," I yell into the phone.

"Say hi," Mom says, and Togo barks. Mom claims Togo recognizes my voice, but I know he's just trained to bark on command. I don't mind, though. After everything today, it feels good to have someone who wants to talk to me. Even if that someone is a dog three thousand miles away in Fairbanks.

I can hear the plinking of the dog food getting poured into Togo's bowl. "I talked to Smiley last night," Mom continues. That's her nickname for Dad because when he was a kid he always had a huge smile. "He told me his and Steph's big news. How you doing with it?"

"Okay, I think. Steph's really nice. How are you doing with it?" I want to know how Mom feels in case it affects how I feel.

"I'm a little sad for myself. For what didn't work out between your dad and me. But I'm also really happy for Smiley. He's such a great guy, and Steph sounds like a good match."

"She's really fun, but she's more of a homebody than you."

"Everyone's more of a homebody than me." Mom laughs. "Smiley told me something else." She pauses. I can tell she's being careful. "Maybe I didn't realize how badly you wanted to get off island."

"I told you what it's been like in school this year."

"I know, but I thought . . . Well, I was certain the tiff between you and Leo would blow over. You were happy before."

"That was before." I bristle.

"Okay, okay." I listen to Togo push his bowl from one side of the kitchen to the other, the metal dish pinging against the baseboards. "I suppose I imagined that if you ever moved again, you might come to live with me."

"In Alaska?"

"Alaska for a couple more years. And then, who knows after that. I could even request something overseas. A big adventure." I can hear the excitement in Mom's voice. I think, for the right person, it would be a great adventure. Learn a new language, live inside a new culture. But for me, right now, that feels like a pull away from something inside my heart. Something I don't yet have a name for.

"Did you always want to leave home?" I ask her.

"It's not so much that I wanted to leave, but I wanted to see new places, experience new things. And I wanted to fly. Even when I was a little kid, I knew that about myself."

"I wish I knew things about myself like you do. Like you did."

"It takes listening to the quiet voice inside you."

"Right now, there are too many loud voices for me to hear my quiet one."

"Tell those loud voices to hush up for a while!" Mom laughs. She has no idea.

Everything feels like it's happening too fast. Dad is coming for me in another eight weeks, and while I know this is what I asked for, what I wanted, I don't know how I'm going to fix everything before I leave. And it's not just that. Not really.

From my window I gaze over the garden. The last of the mountain apples are so deeply red they're almost purple. The taro nearest my window has leaves the shape of giant green hearts. On the warm afternoon breeze the scent of kupaloke is sweet as honey. I'm reminded of why I wanted to move here in the first place. After spending the first eight years of my life bouncing from one town to another because of Mom's job, I wanted a permanent home. Tūtū gave me that. Gave *us*—Dad and me—that. And not just Tūtū. Uncle Kai and my cousins. Leo and his parents. I knew moving to Arizona meant making new friends. I was ready for that. But in talking to Mom, I realize I'm not ready to make a whole new 'ohana.

"I've got to get going," I tell her.

"I love you, baby," she says. And then, as if she remembers suddenly, she adds: "Clara! Not baby. I love you big, mature, thoughtful, getting-to-know-how-to-hear-herself Clara."

"Thanks, Mom. Love you, too."

After the call with Mom, I try to get ahead on my homework. I staple together some paper to make a journal where tomorrow my group and I can track the plants and animals we see, but I don't get any farther than that. I feel too . . . tired.

So instead, I grab my whittling tools and my ʻumeke-in-progress. The center is gouged out, rough, but has taken on the general shape of a bowl. The exterior is kind of wavy—not smooth and perfectly turned like a professional would do. The waves give a sense of movement, though, and I like that. I camp out on the lānai with some rough-grit sandpaper and take to smoothing down the interior.

After a while, I take a break. My wrist needs a little stretch after all the sanding. I stare out over the yard and think of Tūtū listening to her plants. No wonder she can't leave here. Sheʻd miss them, and theyʻd miss her.

Even if I can't hear what the plants are saying, I'll miss them, too. They're familiar to me, like the taste of salt spray on my lips, or the cool of the mountain shadows. And in becoming familiar, the ocean and the land has formed another layer of ʻohana, one that I didn't have before moving here.

A shadow crosses over the grass, and I look up. I can't believe what I see. Etched against the bright sky is a bird with a broad wingspan. It's the 'iwa, come back! I'm sure of it. The 'iwa seems to float in the air, angling ever so slightly for the street. I run through the house to the front yard, and there it is, the wind currents buoying it.

I wish I had thought to grab my binoculars, but there's no time. I follow the 'iwa down the street. It's headed for the mountains, so I jog up the hill, toward the trailhead for the forest reserve. I run past the Boy Scout camp with its huge fleur-de-lis symbol engraved on a sign. Then I scramble over the gate that marks the start of the trail. But now the sky is blocked by trees.

I follow a short dirt path to an asphalt access road that's closed off to traffic. The canopy of trees opens up and I look for the 'iwa, but I can't find it. I run down the road a little, circle back, but no birds fly above me anymore. The leaves of the trees rustle in the wind. A stream nearby chatters. I wait a long time with my face upturned toward the sky, and when at last I give up, dusk is settling over the mountains.

Twenty

THE NEXT MORNING I WAIT for Denny and Titus to arrive. I feel nervous, and Tūtū is making it worse. Every two minutes she's poking her head into my room to ask what kind of snacks Titus and Denny like, or if I want her to drive us anywhere. But her wheezing is so thick that I don't want her to do anything except rest. "Are you feeling okay? Should you be doing that?" I ask, again and again.

But she keeps waving me off. "Tūtū is fine. Just need for move slow."

Finally, gravel crunches beneath car tires in our driveway. Titus has arrived, and Denny is behind him. Tūtū goes out to the porch to meet Denny's mom and Titus's dad. There's a chorus of greetings from us kids: "Hi, Auntie.

Hi, Uncle." And then I usher Titus and Denny through the kitchen and out to the lānai.

"Whoa!" Denny exclaims. "This is major!" I wait for him to think about how tiny the house is, but he doesn't even notice. *If I lived here, I'd camp in this yard every night.*

"You've been holding out on us, Clara," Titus adds.

Denny is carrying a cardboard poster tube under his arm. He pulls off the plastic cap and withdraws a big sheet of paper that he unrolls on the table.

"What is that?"

"A topo map."

"A what map?"

"A topographical map. It's one of the ones from yesterday, but my dad enlarged it at his work." Denny points to a random spot in the middle of the paper. "We're here."

"How do you know?" All I see are scraggly brown and green lines. Some loops, circles. If I didn't know better, I'd say this was geometry class. "What are all these?"

"Kumu Whitman went over this yesterday," Titus says. *You'd know if you were paying attention in class.*

You try to pay attention with twenty boys talking in your head! I want to tell Titus. Instead, I say, "I was distracted."

"Seeing Kumu Apo will do that to you," Denny agrees

158

sympathetically. He points to the paper. "So these loops are elevation lines. A topo map shows the contours of the land, from the highest mountain peak to the lowest valley. Think of it as 3D on a 2D piece of paper." *That's what my dad says to do.*

I try again. The whirls and loops make me feel as if I've crossed my eyes.

"You gotta look at it from a different perspective," Denny coaches. "As if you're a bird looking down."

I guess the shapes are vaguely familiar. "How do you know all this?" I ask Denny.

"My dad and I go hunting a lot. He says I have to learn to read maps, especially if we go to the mainland, because we can't orient to the ocean there."

I am speechless. The class clown is definitely the one earning us an A right now.

Titus marks where we are with a triangle on top of a square—a house symbol. "Did you make an observation journal, Clara?"

"I managed that." I show them the construction paper I stapled around some lined notebook paper.

That's all? Titus thinks.

I frown at Titus. I know my journal isn't as impressive as Denny's map, but his dad helped with that.

"Show us the 'auwai," Denny says. *Let's get moving and focus on our observations.*

I lead them beside the flowing water as it runs from the vegetable garden to the 'ōhi'a trees. "I watch for birds here a lot. And butterflies. Last year a couple Kamehameha butterflies came down here."

Now that is cool, Titus thinks. "I've only seen Kamehameha butterflies in the zoo."

"Apparently in the spring they ascend all the way to the ridges above here. But I've never hiked that high."

For the first entry in our observation journal, we decide to jot down what we see around the 'ōhi'a trees. Denny plops down on the ground while Titus and I remain standing. We have to be quiet in order to see what animals come our way. Only, it's not totally quiet for me.

This ground is pretty damp. Denny shifts around. *Are my shorts getting wet in the 'ōkole?*

I can't help but giggle.

"What are you laughing at?" Denny asks, patting at his backside.

"Nothing," I assure him. "Everything is dry."

He turns bright pink.

"Shhhh," scolds Titus. He points to the grass, where a saffron finch is hopping along.

Denny's thoughts quiet. We all focus on the finch. After a minute, it flies away. Then two zebra doves land on a low branch. We watch the doves coo at each other, and I wonder if any relative of mine has ever been able to listen to birds.

From there we descend to the loʻi. Denny adds details to our map. He traces the ʻauwai and draws a rectangle for each taro patch. Then he adds a tiny kalo over the loʻi that are cultivated and shades the ones that are fallow. Titus points out a dragonfly. Even though it's not a Hawaiian pinao—which would have been really exciting—I sketch it anyway.

When we reach the edge of Tūtū's property, we pause. We can't follow the ʻauwai into my neighbors' yard, so we walk out to the street and down the hill a little, looking for evidence of runoff or water flow.

"Can you imagine what this hillside would have been like a hundred years ago?" Denny asks.

"Or three hundred," Titus adds.

I imagine sandalwood and koa trees blanketing the slope. Yellow ʻamakihi and ʻalauahio trilling among the branches. And the water moving freely. No private property to interfere with its course to the sea.

Titus mops at his forehead with the hem of his T-shirt. "Should we call it? I'm hot."

"What's this area here?" I point to a patch on the

topographical map without any lines.

"I'm not sure," Denny says. "It's down the hill from here but I didn't look up that part."

"Probably the Puʻokinau-o-mahuka heiau," Titus says.

"A heiau here?" Denny says.

"It was a really big one back in the day."

"I'd like to check that out," Denny says. "You up for it?"

"I am," I say. I haven't been there for a few years, probably not since I first moved here.

Titus hauls himself to his feet. "Just tell me one of you brought water."

I offer Titus a water bottle while we walk down to the parking lot for the heiau. When we get there, a sign tells us that this was a luakini heiau, a temple used for sacrifices and rituals tied to success in times of war. The buildings are long gone, of course, but the walls that are still there are made from rough black lava rock that forms three enclosures. From a distance the walls almost look like part of a runway jutting toward the sea. We follow a dirt path that leads around the heiau until we reach an overlook above Waimea Bay and Kamehameha Highway.

"They used to light fires here," Titus explains, "to signal to the heiau in the Wailua district on Kauaʻi. So this heiau is tied to those there."

"How do *you* know that?" Denny asks. It seems like everyone is full of surprises today.

"My auntie from Kaua'i told me. She took me here when she was visiting over the summer."

We stare out over the bay, searching for the outline of Kaua'i in the haze. In the silence, I hear voices whispering, as if they're coming out of the trees that border the overlook. . . . *Jump in the waves and . . . hold your breath . . . get close . . .* I look around, but no one other than Titus and Denny are here. Where are these voices coming from?

"Do you hear that?" says Denny.

"The voices?" Titus asks.

I gulp. How can they be hearing voices, too? Has my gift somehow rubbed off on them? I am starting to panic when suddenly Titus breaks out laughing.

"Is this a trick or something?" Denny growls.

"No trick," Titus says. "With the right wind, you can hear the people on the beach. It's pretty wild, right? My auntie showed me."

"You freaked me out, Titus!" I exclaim. He has no idea how much!

"Can you imagine if you were a kahuna here?" Titus says. "You're a priest and you can hear what the people are saying about you down there."

"I'd totally eavesdrop on the maka'āinana," Denny says. "Then if someone was talking trash about me, I'd know so I could take my revenge."

"I'd use it to be everyone's favorite kahuna." Titus reclines in the shade. The ground is dry here, so Denny and I join him. "If the maka'āinana talked about needing a road or something, I'd build it for them. They'd all love me."

"I wonder if any of them really did amass power that way," Denny muses.

"Or maybe they just listened," I say. "Tried to understand what the people were feeling and thinking."

"Honestly, I don't think I'd want to hear what others are thinking," Titus says. "It's stressful enough talking to them."

"Is that why you're so quiet all the time?" Denny asks. "If you don't talk, you think no one can talk to you?"

"Kind of," Titus says. "It's easy talking with my friends. But with other people . . ."

"You're talking to us. Does that mean we're your friends?" I tease him.

Titus pauses to think, and I realize he's taking my question seriously. "Yeah," he says finally. "Probably."

"We got a 'probably,' Clara. Not bad from this guy." Denny playfully punches Titus in the arm, and Titus socks him back.

Another cool updraft comes off the beach, and the murmurs come with it. I want to try to use my clairboyance again. Even though yesterday was a disaster, maybe this place can be my inspiration, and I can help Denny and Brandon.

I tune into Denny's thoughts. He's got Taylor Swift lyrics running through his head. Is he a Swiftie? Not the point. I've got to get him thinking about Brandon. Then I can get information to help fix their friendship.

"You mind me asking what happened with Kumu Apo yesterday?"

"Don't make me think about it." *Kumu Apo wants us to apologize and hug it out. As if.*

"Let me guess, Kumu Apo wants you to apologize."

"How'd you know?" Denny says glumly. *I bet the kahuna would have punished Brandon.* "Kumu Apo says she's going to bring in our parents if we don't get things figured out on Monday."

"The big guns," Titus quips.

"Exactly." *My dad is going to say to apologize or else, and Brandon's will say to accept it or else. So we'll say what we're supposed to say, but it won't be real. It won't make us friends again.*

"Do you want to be friends with Brandon again?" I ask.

"I guess." Denny shrugs. "If he could stop being such a jerk."

"Sometimes we get caught up in things," I say, remembering yesterday's lunchtime. I was so set on helping Ollie, I didn't notice how my actions were affecting Pua. "You've got to cut people slack. Slow down and listen a little. Learn what's going on for them."

What if I don't want to listen? Denny thinks. I can feel his whole body tense. After a second, though, he relaxes a little. *Maybe Clara isn't totally wrong. I did get caught up in things. I should have backed off even when everyone was yelling at us to fight. Even when Brandon lunged at me.* "I get that I shouldn't have hit Brandon, but he was acting a fool."

"You can't punch someone every time they're acting a fool," says Titus. "I mean, we're all jerks sometimes. Even Clara."

"I'm not a jerk! I didn't mean to hurt Pua's feelings yesterday." If only I hadn't been so focused on Ollie. And here's Titus, throwing it in my face. My eyes well with tears.

"Whoa, I was joking! I wasn't even thinking about yesterday." *This is why I don't like talking. I say stuff like that. I've made Clara cry. She's going to hate me. Why can Denny crack a joke and it sounds fine, and then I open my mouth and it sounds mean?*

166

I take a deep breath, and my eyes clear. "I can't joke about that right now. Pua's ignoring me."

"I'm sorry," he says. "Now I was being the jerk. For what it's worth, I don't think Pua's ignoring you. She's going through some stuff."

"What kind of stuff?"

"On the bus, she told me her closest friend is about to move off island. Can you believe it? Pua moves all this way, and then her friend takes off."

"Oh, Titus," I sigh. I feel grateful that Pua called me her closest friend. She's my closest friend these days, too. But I'm also sad. Here we are, two months from my leaving, and we're not even talking. What kind of friendship is that? "I don't think she moved to be close to someone," I say finally. "I think she made a close friend who's leaving soon."

"Aren't you leaving soon, Clara?" Denny says.

"Waaaait." Titus gasps. "Are you the friend?"

I nod. "My dad's going to pack me up over Christmas break."

"Shoot," Titus says. "I kind of liked eating with you and Pua. You even made Nalu loosen up."

"Yeah, Clara," Denny agrees. "Even the voices of the heiau think you should stick around. Listen."

We all fall silent. The voices from the beach surge

around us. Murmurs and whispers and tremors. "Don't go," I hear one of the voices say. "Don't go," calls another. When I stand up to peek over the cliff, I see Titus and Denny with their hands cupped around their mouths. They're laughing, but I know they're sincere. After all, I can hear what they're thinking. *Don't go, Clara. Don't leave for Arizona.*

Twenty-One

LATER IN THE AFTERNOON, AFTER Titus and Denny have gone home, I add more to our observation log. I describe the wind at Puʻokinau-o-mahuka and draw the clouds that formed over the sea. It feels like learning a place is endless, like there's always another observation to make, another way to see and hear and feel one's home.

In her bedroom, I hear the whir of Tūtū's nebulizer. She uses the nebulizer to break down her asthma medicine into a fine mist that she can more easily inhale. I knew she was feeling wheezy, but I didn't realize she was nebulizer-level wheezy.

"You need anything?" I ask when I poke my head in her bedroom.

Usually when she's on her machine she'll point me to

whatever she wants—a magazine, the TV remote. Then, while the medicine works its magic and helps open her airways, I hang out doing homework or reading or eating a snack. Afterward she might want to lie down and rest, but she can always talk to me and her wheezing always lessens. This afternoon, though, she doesn't point at anything. She just waves me away, signaling nothing is needed.

I hesitate, not sure if I should leave her alone. She lifts the mask off her face and a white puff of aerosolized medicine dissipates in front of her. "I fine," she says tightly. "Go on."

I leave her door ajar so I can hear if she calls. I thought we'd work in the lo'i this afternoon, but it's clear that Tūtū isn't up for that. And I don't know if I should text Pua about hanging out. Before Titus came over, I was certain Pua didn't want to talk to me. Now I wonder if she wants me to check in.

Still on for this weekend? I text her.

I wait several minutes and when there's no answer, I throw myself onto my bed. A sharp corner pokes into me. Under my quilt is the whittling book that Steph got for me. Now that I'm finished with my 'umeke, I should think of another project. I thumb through the pages. A turtle. A garden gnome. I pause on a pattern for a comfort bird—a bird figurine that's sanded smooth to the touch and has no details. It's called a comfort bird because it feels good sitting in your hand. That sounds kind of nice. I could use a little comfort.

I think of Titus and his anxiety talking to people he's not close with, or Denny and his upcoming meeting with Brandon. Seems like I'm not the only one who could use a comfort bird.

Across the hall, Tūtū's nebulizer clicks off. She must have run through the medicine. I'm sure she'll be feeling better in no time. The sun and wind at the heiau have tired me out. I decide to rest my eyes for a minute. At least until Tūtū says she's ready to get things done in the loʻi.

When I open my eyes again, the light outside my window has shifted, and my room feels stuffy and hot. It's late afternoon. I've been asleep for a couple of hours. I'm surprised to hear the soft growl of Tūtū's nebulizer echoing down the hall. It's unlike her to do two sessions so close together—usually it would be another six hours before she'd use the machine again.

I get out of bed and tiptoe down the hall. She's left her bedroom and is seated at the everything table, the clear mask over her nose and mouth. When she sees me, she raises her eyebrows as if to ask, *Where have you been?*

I pat down my hair, all wild from my nap.

Her breaths come in shallow sips. Even with the machine and medicine, she doesn't seem to be getting much air. "You okay?" I ask.

She doesn't answer. She doesn't even make eye contact.

I don't want to leave her, but I don't want her to think I'm hovering either. Tūtū can be touchy about her asthma. So I curl up on the couch and thumb through a magazine. But her shallow breathing is really worrying me. The last time Tūtū was this bad she had to go to the hospital. Dad actually called the paramedics and rode with her while Leo and Auntie Nina came to stay with me.

Now I text him. *Tūtū's using her nebulizer for the second time in two hours. Should I be worried?*

He texts right back. *How she sound?*

I listen to her rasping breath, the rattle deep in her chest. *Not good*, I type. *Rattly.*

Should I call her?

The last thing Tūtū needs is Dad stressing her out when she's having an attack. *Not now.*

On machine still?

Yes.

Ask how bad on a scale 1-10. Above 7, call me.

When this happened before, not long after we moved back, Dad explained how a hospital nebulizer is stronger and better able to move medicine to the lungs. Even though it can feel scary to see someone hooked up to tubes, it's also a sign of how much help they're receiving. It's a chance to be grateful.

"Tūtū," I say loud enough to be heard over the nebulizer. "How many sessions have you done today?"

She holds up three fingers. She must have done one while I was down at the heiau.

"That seems like a lot. Does it feel like it's helping?"

She doesn't nod or shake her head, and I realize if she has to think about the answer, that means it's not helping enough.

"On a scale of one to ten . . . ," I start.

She holds up nine fingers.

I need to do more than dial Dad. "Tūtū, should I call 9-1-1?"

"Where you go?" she manages to huff.

"I'll go to Leo's." It's instinct, really, that makes me say his name. Who else would I turn to when I need help?

Tūtū nods again, this time more slowly, like she's making a decision. I think of Mom talking about listening to the quiet inner voice. Maybe for Tūtū and me, who are surrounded by others' voices all the time, it can be hard to hear that voice, but it's also totally vital to listen for it.

"Call," she says finally.

So, I dial. When the operator picks up, I try to keep my voice steady, though it shakes anyway. I tell her my tūtū is having a bad asthma attack and can't breathe. I tell her she's used her nebulizer three times today but it's not helping. I tell her Tūtū needs to go to the hospital but can't drive herself.

The operator asks me how old Tūtū is. "In her sixties," I say. For a second, I worry the operator will ask where my parents are, but she doesn't. She asks me to very clearly tell her our address, and I do. Then she tells me the paramedics are on their way.

"Do you want me to stay on the line until they arrive?" she asks.

I do, but I don't want to seem like a little kid who needs that, so I tell her that I'm okay. "Thank you," I say before I hang up.

"Ten minutes," I report to Tūtū. She's off the machine now and trying to stay focused on inhaling, getting little sips of air. I sit next to her. Her eyes are closed. I'm afraid if I look away, she'll die.

Soon enough I hear ambulance sirens in the distance.

"Show them," Tūtū huffs. "Here."

I run outside and wave my arms on the front lawn so the paramedics don't have to search for an address. They pull into the driveway and hop out of the ambulance. "My tūtū is in the living room," I say. There are three of them. The driver and two EMTs, one of whom grabs a kit and another who is carrying a portable nebulizer. "She's been using her machine all day," I tell the woman with the nebulizer.

"Good to know," she says. "Thanks."

Once they're inside, I press myself against the wall. There's two of them bustling around with their kits and machines and equipment. They take Tūtū's pulse, listen to her chest with a stethoscope. They ask her age (sixty-four) and when this attack started (around ten a.m.).

"But how long you been feeling bad, Auntie?" the woman with the nebulizer asks.

"Two days," Tūtū says.

Two days! I knew Tūtū was wheezy, but I didn't realize she'd been feeling bad. I wish she wouldn't have hidden this from me. What if I was still down at the heiau with the guys? Who would have taken care of her then?

The EMTs put a mask over her face and hook it into an

oxygen tank. They tell me they need to take her to Kahuku Medical Center to get her to the help she needs. "You going to be okay?" asks the EMT quietly. "You have folks to look after you?"

"M-my friend," I stutter. "I'll go there."

They put Tūtū on a stretcher with wheels that drop down at the press of a button and steer her to the ambulance. I follow behind with her purse. Before they lift her into the back, I give her a kiss on her forehead. She pulls the oxygen mask off her face. "Call Dad," she manages to say. The back door of the ambulance closes.

Through the back window I can see the EMTs moving around Tūtū. There are oxygen tubes and IVs and monitors with bleeping lights. She looks small inside all that. Is she going to be okay? Am I?

Then the ambulance is driving away, the back window too distant to peer into. They turn a corner, and before I know it, Tūtū is gone.

Twenty-Two

I'M SHAKING SO BADLY I have to sit down on the dirt driveway. My body no longer seems my own. Once, when we lived in Texas, the paramedics came to a neighbor's house, and afterward everyone went over to check on the family. But out here, our neighbors are all the way down the road. If they're not home, then no one will see the ambulance. I'm all alone.

I manage to stumble inside, to the couch. I'm shivering, as if I've never been this cold in my whole life. I pull a quilt around my shoulders and fumble for my phone. Dad has called twice and left a string of worried texts. I have to call him back but I need someone who can be here with me now, in person. I find Auntie Nina in my phone. She picks up on the second ring.

"Clara! I haven't heard from you for a long time. Everything okay?" Her voice is too low, too careful. She must sense that something's wrong. Why else would I call after all these months?

"It's Tūtū," I manage to say. "She went to the hospital." And then the waterworks come. I can't hold them back anymore. I'm sobbing and hiccuping so hard it takes me a minute to tell Auntie Nina it's an asthma attack. That I have nowhere to go.

"Oh, Clara, I come for get you right now. You always have one place with us. You know that." I hear keys jingle in the background. "You call your dad yet? You want me to?"

"I'll call him," I say.

"You sure? We can call when I get there. I can stay on the line while I drive to you."

Knowing she's on her way is enough to stop my tears. "That's okay, Auntie. I feel better now. I'll call my dad when I hang up with you."

"Okay, I'll be there in eight minutes. I going to set a new record." As if to prove her point, Auntie Nina's engine revs loudly.

When I get off the phone with her, I call Dad.

"Paramedics?!" he exclaims when I tell him what's happened. I hear him repeating what I said to Steph.

"Are they okay? You need to fly out there?" Steph's voice reaches the upper octaves.

"Yeah, I think I need to fly out," he tells her.

"Dad, last time this happened you said not to worry. The hospital had the equipment to fix everything."

"I know I said that. But last time I was there. She wasn't alone. And neither were you." Dad takes a few long, deep breaths over the phone. "I should be with you. You shouldn't have to do something like this on your own." There's a rustle, and soft murmuring between him and Steph. I can't make out what they're saying, probably because Dad is muffling the phone. When he returns, he sounds a little calmer. "The soonest I can get in is tomorrow afternoon. Steph's booking the flight."

"Okay. I'll tell Auntie Nina."

"Auntie Nina?"

"I called her before I called you."

"Oh." My dad pauses. "You called her first?"

"She's on her way."

"Good. That's good." His voice trembles a little. "And you're okay hanging out with Leo?"

"It'll be fine." At least I hope it will be.

"Well, think of it as a farewell tour."

"What do you mean, 'farewell tour'?"

"This is a wake-up call for me," Dad says. "When I get there, I'm going to pack you up for Arizona. And Tūtū, too, if she'll let me. It's the only right thing to do."

"Pack me up now? Christmas is still two months away."

"That's too far. When I fly back, you'll come with me. I'm going to move you next week."

I'm speechless. I'm not ready to move next week. I just started working on fixing things with Denny and Brandon. And I'm nowhere near clearing up the mess with Pua. And the loʻi needs me. And there's still Leo. . . .

"Dad, that's too soon!"

"I know it's fast. But under the circumstances, I can't think of another option."

"Tūtū will never let this happen."

"I'll talk to her. After this, she's going to understand. She loves you as much as I do."

"But, Dad, I can't—"

"Clara? Are you there?" Auntie Nina's voice interrupts the phone call. She knocks at the front screen door.

"Is that Nina?" Dad asks.

When I open the door to her, Auntie Nina sweeps me into a big hug. It's been so long since I've seen her—six months or more. She's cropped her hair short, and she's wearing a bright red lipstick. She looks different. Less casual mom and more model. But her hug is exactly the same. Two squeezes and a kiss on top of the head.

"I missed you," she murmurs into my hair.

"I missed you, too," I say.

Dad's voice echoes out of my cell phone. "Nina? Is that you? Clara, can you put Nina on?" I hand my phone to her.

My head is spinning. It feels like my heart is, too. I don't understand why Dad is suddenly in a rush for me to move. I handled everything with Tūtū. And if I wasn't here, who would have taken care of her? I called the paramedics. I found a place to go for myself. What did I do wrong?

Next to me, Auntie Nina and Dad are talking logistics. What hospital Tūtū is at. What time Dad's flight gets in. Dad thinks he's telling her the most important details, but he's leaving out what really matters: We're moving away. We're not planning on coming back. And if Tūtū doesn't agree to come, then she'll be all by herself. The thought makes me feel like the floor has dropped out from under me.

I lean on the everything table. Tūtū's nebulizer is next to a pile of mail. Quilt squares have been pushed to the edge. I can smell the scent of her acrid medication mixing with the sweetness of flowers blooming in the humid afternoon heat. This is what home smells like to me.

After Dad and Auntie Nina hang up, she helps me pack

an overnight bag and my homework. I feel like a zombie, wandering through the house, not remembering where I left my books. How can I be moving next week? How will I fix everything before I leave? How do I make sure Tūtū is going to be okay?

Auntie Nina is so calm, so level-headed. She reminds me to leave a porch light on. She checks that the back door is locked, even though Tūtū never locks the back door. In Phoenix, Dad and Steph lock up the apartment when they're only running downstairs to grab the mail. Finally, Auntie Nina locks up the front. As we walk out to the car, I realize there's someone sitting in it.

Leo!

I stop in my tracks, turn to Auntie. "Leo's here?"

"He asked to come. It's okay, yeah?" She looks at me searchingly. For the first time, I wonder what Auntie Nina knows about Leo and me. She must have realized something changed. She hasn't seen me forever. But what has Leo told her?

I drop my overnight bag and backpack in the trunk. I move slowly, nervous to get in the car. What's it going to be like seeing Leo? Will he still be mad at me about yesterday? And why did he ask to come?

As soon as I open the back door, Leo's thoughts come

rushing out. *Is Tūtū okay? Does Clara want me here? Is she going to act normal? Am I?* Somewhere in that barrage he manages to say, "Hi."

I want to tell him that I'm glad he's here. That for all our awkwardness, it's reassuring to see him. That he and his mom make me feel steady. But instead of all that, I reply, "Hi."

I slide into the back seat. He gives me a smile. I smile back. Then he pulls off his ball cap and tucks it under his arm. *Better safe than sorry.*

Oh no! Even in this moment, he doesn't trust me. I buckle up, but I can't look at him anymore.

Auntie Nina's phone buzzes. "We can go to the hospital now."

"The hospital?" Leo repeats. *No way. I thought we were just picking Clara up.*

"Uncle Koa texted. Tūtū is already out of ER and in her own room. We can visit."

I never want to go to a hospital ever again. I came to make sure Clara was okay. Leo is twirling his curls at top speed. *I don't want to smell that hospital smell.*

I hadn't thought what it might be like for Leo to have to go into a hospital. How it might bring up memories of his dad's illness.

"You folks don't have to come in," I say. "I don't mind going alone."

"Don't be silly," Auntie Nina replies. "We like come with you."

I don't want to see the tubes and machines.

"Maybe Leo doesn't have to come in," I say, wanting to help him out.

Yeah, maybe I don't have to. He sighs, releases his curls. But after a minute, he goes back to spinning his hair. *I would like to see Tūtū. Let her know I'm thinking of her.*

As we drive into Kahuku, we pass the famous shrimp trucks. I roll my window down to let the air in. Phoenix has some pretty awesome food trucks, but none where the scent of garlic mixes with the sweet brine of the ocean.

Maybe Tūtū will be better and we can take her home with us?

I want to tell Leo that I'd like that, too.

Once Auntie Nina has parked, she asks Leo, "You want to come in?"

"Um, well . . ." *Not really, but I do want to see Tūtū.*

"Leo can stay in the car," I suggest.

"It's too hot in the car," Auntie says.

I know what to expect, and Clara could use my—

"Or the lobby. Leo could hang there."

184

Wait, what's happening? Does Clara not want me there?

No! I *do* want Leo there. I was trying to be kind and help him avoid going in the hospital!

"I'll wait on the benches outside." He sounds so defeated. I don't know how I messed that up. I was trying to solve things for him.

Leo finds a spot near the entrance. "Tell Tūtū I love her, 'kay?" he says to his mom. Auntie Nina blows him a kiss.

Inside the hospital, Auntie Nina talks to the main desk to find out what room Tūtū is in. When the receptionist asks if we need directions, Auntie shakes her head no. She knows the way. I wonder if it's hard for her to be here, too.

Auntie Nina leads us from one corridor to another. At a nurse's desk she pauses, chats for a moment, and then motions to a narrow hall lined with doors. "She's down here," Auntie Nina says. I'm nervous as we walk along the hallway. Almost all the doors are open, but behind them are curtains pulled to give people privacy. Part of me is afraid there's blood and guts behind those curtains, but the other part of me knows it's just people resting as they heal. A white-haired woman pushing a walker passes me in the hallway and smiles. In one room a man is practicing rotating his shoulder and laughing with a nurse. I feel reassured by what I see. But maybe I'm different from Leo in that way.

I pause in front of Tūtū's room. Will she look like herself? "You want me come in with you?" Auntie Nina asks.

"Um, maybe I'll go in first."

"I can wait right here."

I take a deep breath and remind myself that the not-knowing is the hard part. Then I step around the curtain.

Tūtū is napping. She has a clear plastic mask over her nose and mouth with tubing that runs to an oxygen machine. She's also hooked up to one of those monitors that tracks her heartbeat. The machine doesn't beep, though, not like the ones in the movies.

Her arms are bare and the faded hospital gown is tied around her neck. I see the loose skin, the wrinkles. Tūtū looks old, and for a moment I'm scared. But then Tūtū opens her eyes and sits up. The wrinkles smooth as she gives me a big smile. She pulls the mask off her face. "There's the Shrub!"

"Eh, Tūtū. Shouldn't you leave that on?"

"You sound like one nurse," she teases, but she puts the mask back over her face. Her voice is steady even if the wheezing is still thick.

"You sound better."

"Feel better, too." She points to a chair in the corner of the room. "Pull it up. Stay awhile."

"Auntie Nina is in the hall."

"Ooh, let me freshen up."

Tūtū runs her fingers through her hair and pulls the blanket up over her chest. I like watching her fuss over her appearance a little. It makes her seem like her old self.

When Auntie Nina comes in, she embraces Tūtū and gently kisses her cheek. "You okay?"

Tūtū tilts her head in a way that says yes and no. "Worried about Clara. But now that you're here, I not."

"You should have went call me when you started feeling bad," Auntie Nina scolds gently.

"Didn't know how bad it was going to get."

Auntie kisses Tūtū on the cheek one more time and then settles back in one of the chairs I've pulled up.

"Where's Leo? At home?" Tūtū asks.

"Outside," Auntie answers. "He wasn't up for coming in."

Tūtū nods like she understands.

"Dad tell you he's flying out?" I ask Tūtū.

"He didn't say that."

"He comes tomorrow afternoon."

"Overreacting, him!"

187

I bite my lip. Should I tell her his plan to move me? I decide to wait. No need to upset her when she's recovering.

"He wants an excuse to see you." Auntie Nina pats Tūtū's hand. Of course she'd say that. She doesn't know about Dad's plan either.

Tūtū and Auntie Nina talk story for a few minutes. Tūtū notices the new haircut. "Looks good on you," she tells Auntie Nina.

"Thought I'd try something new."

"You been doing okay? Long time, we never talk." Tūtū peers over her glasses at Auntie Nina, and something unsaid passes between them.

"Hard figuring out who you are after losing someone," Auntie Nina says.

"Real hard," Tūtū agrees. "It doesn't happen overnight. Little by little." This time it's Tūtū who reaches out for Auntie Nina, and the two hold hands. "But hey, I need a few minutes with my Shrub."

Auntie Nina gives Tūtū's hand a squeeze and releases it. "I see you real soon, okay?"

"Thank you for caring for my girl."

"Anytime. You know that." Auntie Nina blows Tūtū a kiss as she leaves the room.

When we're alone, Tūtū asks, "Everything go okay with the boys this morning?"

"It was really fun, actually." I tell her about showing Denny and Titus our loʻi and how beautiful they thought it was. I describe going down to the heiau and the voices that came up from the beach. I even tell her about the conversation Denny and I had, and how I'm hoping maybe it will help him hear out Brandon on Monday.

"I'm happy for all this, Shrub. Sounds like you getting better at using your clairboyance." She beams at me.

"Kind of," I say. "With Leo, it's different. Like, on the way here, I tried to make it so he didn't have to come inside the hospital. But I think I made things worse for him."

"Eh, maybe you need for take your own advice. Like you told the boys up at the heiau. Sometimes better for slow down and listen."

"But listening isn't exactly an action. It doesn't make things happen!" Tūtū doesn't understand. I'm on a time-line here. The clock is ticking, and I've got a week to make things better.

"I just saying. Trying for force things is never the way for solve a problem."

Tūtū nestles back in her pillows. She's tired. She tells

189

me to help out Auntie Nina while I'm staying with them and not to worry about her. She's getting good care. When I lean over the bed railing to give Tūtū a hug, I press my ear to her chest. I listen to her lungs whistle and wheeze. I listen to her strong heart go thump-thump-thump. "Shrub," she whispers, "when you go listening, listen to your own heart, too. Plenty answers in there."

Twenty-Three

I FOLLOW THE BIG ARROWS back to the lobby. Leo and his mom are sitting next to each other on a bench outside the sliding doors. His head is resting on her shoulder, and her head is leaned on his. I hesitate to interrupt them, but Auntie Nina must hear me. "You ready to go?" she says, before turning to face me.

"When you folks are."

"How was Tūtū?" Leo asks.

"Much better. If you want to come up next time, I'd like that."

"Okay." *I could have come up this time. But next time is okay, too.*

I hang my head. Next time I won't rush into fixing things.

Once we're in the car, Auntie Nina asks if we want plate lunch from Ted's Bakery.

"And pie?" Leo asks.

Auntie laughs. "I knew you'd say that."

At the bakery, we order our usual. Teri beef for me, chicken katsu for Leo. Auntie Nina buys a whole chocolate haupia pie. "You can take the leftovers home to your dad," she tells me.

"There's not going to be leftovers." Leo laughs and winks at me.

Once, at a barbecue at Leo's house, when his dad was still living, he and I ate a whole pie before dinner. The adults didn't even notice until they went to get it from the fridge. Now it's a story everyone likes to tell. A funny thing that happened back in the day when we were all together.

Our takeout makes the whole car smell good, and for the rest of the ride we mostly talk about how hungry we are. We remember other good meals, too. The best ribs Uncle Will ever grilled. The biggest fish Dad and Uncle Kai ever caught. (If only they knew how Uncle Kai always caught the best fish!) Mom's famous liliko'i cheesecake recipe. We're drooling by the time Auntie Nina steers the car into Waialua. And Leo and me, well, it almost feels like old times.

The moment we park in front of Leo and Auntie Nina's house, other memories come flooding back. There are happy ones, like when Leo's parents threw us a big welcome-home party after Dad and I moved back, and sad ones, like when Leo's parents told him that Uncle Will's cancer had come back. There are fuzzy ones that I don't quite remember from when Leo and I were really little and Mom, Dad, and I only visited the islands at Christmas. And there are sharp ones, where I remember every detail, like Dad showing Leo how to hold his first 'ukulele.

What I don't have are memories from these past months, so I notice all the little changes. A new chair on the porch. A fresh coat of paint on the front door. The photographs on a side table rearranged to make room for Leo's sixth-grade school portrait.

In the kitchen, Auntie Nina unpacks the takeout. "Grab yourself something to drink," she tells me. "You know where everything is."

The soda and bubbly water are still in the fridge in the garage. The chopsticks are still in a jar on a kitchen counter. I hand Leo a stack of napkins, and he sets the table without saying anything. It's nice to feel old rhythms kick in.

Auntie Nina says grace, and then we dig into our dinner.

"I'm looking forward to seeing your dad," Auntie Nina says. "Been too long."

"He'll be happy to see you folks."

"And how are he and Steph? Things going good there?"

"They got engaged."

"Engaged?" Auntie Nina exclaims. "Wow. Hoʻomaikaʻi!"

"Like, engaged to get married?" Leo says. *Is Clara cool with that?*

"It's all good," I say. "Steph's really nice. Plus, she's a local girl."

"Maui, right? Where Steph grew up?" Auntie Nina asks.

"Yeah, Maui."

"They like come home, then? Your dad and Steph?"

"Um, well, actually—" I want to tell them I'm moving but it's hard to build up to it.

"What'd your mom say when she found out?" Leo jumps in. *Was she jealous? Uncle Koa moving on without her?*

"She said Steph seems like a good match for him."

For real? She didn't get mad? Or sad? Or want things to go back—

"She said she was a little sad, but mostly happy." Oof. Should have let Leo finish his thought. But I want him to know my mom is okay. "She called Dad 'Smiley' so I think she was telling the truth."

"Your mom," Auntie Nina says. "She never one for hide her feelings. Not like you and your dad. Quiet on the surface but underneath big things happening."

"Yeah, big things." I take a deep breath. Now's my chance to tell them about the move. "So next week Dad is—"

"He'll be here for my last Little League game," Leo interjects. *Perfect timing! For the play-offs, too.* "You think he can come?"

"Um, well, he'll be pretty busy."

"He's got Tūtū to think of," Auntie Nina joins in. "We can ask, but don't get your hopes up."

I won't. But maybe if he comes, Clara will come and it will be like old times. And we can—

"I'm moving to Arizona." There. I said it. I got it out.

"What?" *WHAT?!?!*

"What?" echoes Auntie Nina. "I mean, when?" She drops her chopsticks she's so flustered. I didn't realize the news would affect her this way.

"Dad wants me to go back with him. Like, next week."

Whoa, whoa, whoa. Stop. That's too soon. This is all too soon.

"That's fast," Auntie Nina says. "What did Tūtū say?"

"She doesn't know my dad wants it to happen right away."

If Tūtū doesn't know yet, then it won't happen. It can't.

She'll never let Uncle Koa move Clara. She's too stubborn. Too paʻakikī.

"When did he make this decision?" Auntie Nina carefully wipes the rice she dropped, each kernel into her napkin. Her eyes are downcast.

"I asked to move at Christmas. He sped up the timeline."

"So, you like go?" Auntie Nina's face softens. I can tell she's trying really hard to be happy for me.

Clara asked! I should have known! She liked the mainland so much, she wants to go live there. She'll even ditch me to do it.

"I think so," I answer Auntie Nina. But what I want to say is: I don't know anymore. I'm not sure. It's all happening too fast. I'm starting to like my life here again, and tonight with her and Leo is making it harder to imagine living anywhere other than . . . home.

"Can I be excused, Mom?" Leo asks. *I'm done here.*

"Leo, we're still eating."

Come on, let me go. Let me have, like, some time.

"I don't mind, Auntie," I say.

"Okay," she relents. "But, Leo, you're on dish duty in a half hour."

Leo is out of there so fast I can't even catch a thought before he's gone. But what lingers in his place is a deep sense of sadness. I can't help wondering: Is it his, or is it mine?

I poke at my mac salad. Suddenly I'm not hungry anymore.

"Help me clear the table?" Auntie Nina asks softly.

We stack our unfinished dinners in the fridge. Leo managed to wolf all of his down before I dropped my announcement, so at least he won't be sad *and* hungry. I wipe down the table while Auntie runs hot water for the dishes. Their house doesn't have a dishwasher either. One of those funny little things that used to make it feel like Leo and I were destined to be lifelong besties.

"I know you and Leo haven't been as close recently," Auntie Nina says finally. "Friend groups change, that kine thing."

Well, Leo had a group. I had a hiding spot behind the cafeteria. But I don't say that. I wait, listen.

"And I haven't reached out like I should. Check up on you and Tūtū." She leans heavily against the sink. "Sometimes it's hard, you know? You get so focused on figuring out your next step." Auntie runs her fingers through her short hair. "You forget everyone else is trying to figure out theirs, too."

"I know what you mean." I sigh.

Auntie holds her arms out to me, and I go in for the hug.

Two squeezes and a kiss on the head. "You kids, getting big so fast," she murmurs into my hair. When she releases me, she wipes at her eyes. "You go find Leo for me?"

I gulp. I don't really want to go find Leo. I bet he's mad at me. But Auntie Nina clearly needs a few minutes to herself.

"I think he's in the guest bedroom," she says. "Tell him to set up the futon for you."

Guest bedroom? Since when do they have a guest bedroom?

I wander into the hall. Leo's bedroom door is open but he's not there. Instead, I hear a rhythmic slapping noise in his dad's office.

He's sitting in the desk chair, tossing a baseball into the air and catching it.

"So this is the guest bedroom?" I ask.

"I still call it the office." *Mom's the one who wanted to call it something different.*

"The room looks the same." There's still a desk and a computer, still a row of ball caps lining a display shelf on the wall.

He notices where I'm looking. "Maybe don't touch those," he says. *Can I trust Clara in here? Can I trust her with anything?*

I hang my head. Of course he can trust me! But I get

why he doesn't know that. I still haven't apologized for yesterday, and right when we were getting back on track, I dropped the news that I'm moving.

"Did Mom say to get out the futon?" *Let's get this done and over with. Then I can go to my room and be left alone.*

I feel sad hearing what he's thinking. Old me would have retreated to the bathroom. But new me—me with clairboyance, me with only a few days left—knows that I have to talk to Leo. Should I hand him my apology note? Launch into saying I'm sorry?

Leo is struggling to pull the futon mattress out of the closet.

Okay, maybe I should start by helping him with that. "Here," I say, grabbing the other end. We maneuver the heavy mattress to the middle of the room. It's Japanese style, the kind you unroll on the floor. Super comfortable but not very lightweight.

"Is this the one from your room?" Auntie Nina used to store it under Leo's bed.

"Same one." *More space in here now that Dad's stuff is gone.* "I'll grab you clean sheets."

While Leo is searching for sheets in the hall closet, I take another look at the room. In the first year after Uncle Will died, nothing changed around the house. But it seems like, in the past six months, a lot has. The desk is clearer now without Uncle Will's stack of invoices. His toolbox is gone from the floor. A chair where he used to pile his work clothes has been removed and in its place is a plant stand holding a potted fern. I wonder what this fern would tell Tūtū if she were here.

I take a step toward the shelf of hats. Uncle Will got these for Leo. A cap from every ballpark they'd ever visited. Most are from California—the Angels, the Dodgers, the Oakland A's—but a couple are from farther travels. Like the Astros' cap, which Uncle Will got when he, Auntie, and Leo came to visit us in Texas.

"What are you doing?!" Leo's voice makes me jump.

"Just looking," I promise.

"Well, don't do that." *Not after yesterday.*

"Sorry," I answer snappishly. Then I take a deep breath. I want him to know I'm genuinely sorry. About a lot of things. "I'm sorry about yesterday. About your Giants hat."

I don't want to talk about it. He busies himself unfolding a sheet.

I press my lips together. If he doesn't want to talk, then maybe I shouldn't speak. I did tell myself I'd listen. But the silence is too much. "I was trying to get your attention, and I got carried away."

Leo looks up from the pillowcase he's been trying to stuff with an oversized throw pillow. *Why would Clara want my attention? After months of avoiding me, why yesterday?*

"Michelle asked me to help her. Make you pay attention to her."

I knew it. Clara didn't really want to talk to me herself.

"I did want to talk to you!"

"Huh?" *How did Clara know what I was thinking?*

I told myself I wouldn't talk, and instead I full-on conversed with Leo's thoughts. But now I'm in too deep. I have to say something more. "I mean, I would have wanted to talk to you myself. If I had known you wanted to talk to me."

"Why wouldn't I want to talk to you?"

"Because of the beginning of the school year. When you ruined my sketchbook."

"I didn't mean to! Honest." In frustration, Leo throws the pillow onto the futon. *Can't Clara let this go? It was an accident. I apologized. Why is she still mad at me?* "I said that in my note."

"What note?"

"The one Michelle delivered for me."

Wait—I never got a note from Leo. And Michelle definitely didn't deliver anything to me. "Michelle delivered it for you?"

"I couldn't exactly go into the girls' bathroom where you were camped out." *What does Clara want from me?*

I want to know what he's talking about! But I can see that hearing his thoughts isn't enough, I need a more complete picture. Because clearly we are not remembering the same thing.

I look around the room. If I can hold on to something with meaning to him, something with memories, then maybe I'll understand. The ball caps sit colorfully on their shelf. I know what I need to do.

"Do you mind asking your mom for a different pillow?" I smile sweetly.

"Yeah, sure. I don't know why she wants all these decorative ones anyway." He stomps out of the room.

As soon as he's gone, I approach the shelf. What hat did he wear the first day of school? I have to remember. Blue. It was definitely blue. I look at each one by one and—yes! The Mariners. I know Leo told me not to touch any of these, but I have to. I have to know what note he's talking about.

I pat the hat gently, wait for a memory to appear. *Come on*, I think. I need to see this memory before Leo returns. But there's nothing. I rub my hand over the yellow "S" logo. Still nothing. I can hear him talking to his mom. I don't have much longer. I need to make this work. So I snatch up the hat and plop it on my head, and then—

The cafeteria is echoing with voices. Everyone is excited for the first day of school. My sketchbook is on the table. I'm pointing to a drawing of a Ferris wheel in Vegas. Showing off a sketch of snakeskin cowboy boots. I'm saying that my dad promised to buy me a pair like them. That maybe I'll become a cowgirl.

Denny cracks a joke. Everyone laughs. Except Leo. He wants me to stop talking about my trip. Stop talking about how great it is over there.

Michelle says, "If you love the mainland so much, go back there already!"

"You know, she's kind of right, Clara," Leo says glumly.

I know all this part. I lived it, too. What I didn't know is that Leo is mad at me. That's why he sounds so down. He's mad that I might leave him.

When I stand, I push the table away. He sees the milk carton tottering, and tries to reach it, but his fingers graze the side. It's tipping. He can't stop it, but he wants to. Suddenly, the milk is everywhere. My sketchbook is soaked.

And then I hear everything from Leo's perspective. Denny and Brandon cracking some jokes. Laughter that is muffled.

He doesn't even look up. He feels terrible. He knows I'm going to be upset. He thinks that now, for sure, I'm going to move to the mainland.

I'm fleeing. But this time, I watch myself go. Leo is watching me go, and he's scared. Scared of losing me.

At the end of the lunch period, Michelle tells him I'm hiding in the girls' bathroom, so he writes me a note. Gives it to Michelle to deliver. But I never say a word about it. I never say anything to him. Don't even answer his text. I just look right through him as if he doesn't exist.

The memory fades. I hear footsteps in the hall and quickly I pull the hat off my head, but it's still in my hands when Leo returns.

"I told you not to touch them!"

"I know, but I had to see—" I stop myself. How do I explain that I had to see his memories? "I had to see that this one was okay still. That, um, no milk got on it." I shake my head. That sounded so random!

He reaches for the hat, and I hand it to him. I wonder if he'll be angry. Instead, he thinks: *I haven't worn this one since . . . since Clara and I were still friends.* "Did you really never get my note?" The questions is directed at the Mariners hat, but I get that it's for me.

I shake my head. "Tell me what it said."

"That I was sorry about spilling the milk on your sketchbook." *I wanted you to forgive me. I wanted things to be okay between us again.*

"And you trusted Michelle to give it to me? I mean, she has a crush—" I stop myself. This is my chance to get back at Michelle. To make Leo stop hanging out with her.

But is that what this is about? Is that what I want this to be about?

"She has a crushing fear of public restrooms," I say. "It would have been very hard for her to get it to me."

Leo gives me a funny look, but then he shrugs. "I had no idea." He lets out a long sigh. "I thought you wanted to leave. You had had so much fun on the mainland. Plus, your mom lives off island, now your dad. What's keeping you from ditching me?"

"I don't want to ditch you!" I don't want to leave Leo or Auntie Nina or Oʻahu at all. And I'm terrified that Tūtū could end up by herself. "It's just, you made this whole new crew, and until Pua showed up I was totally on my own. You even let them make fun of me. Call me names. You're the one who ditched me."

There's a long silence. Maybe Leo is too shocked to talk or even think. Maybe he's mad at me. Maybe I shouldn't have said anything. But then he hangs his head low. Faintly, so faintly I can barely make out the thought: *Clara is right.*

I can't believe what I'm hearing.

I wanted to be tight with them so badly. First, Brandon and Denny. Then when Michelle and Crystal started hanging out with us. I thought . . . I thought . . .

"Tell me what you were thinking!"

"I thought that if I was tight with them, then it would be okay if you left."

"But I didn't want to leave! Not until our friendship was over."

"So, our friendship is over?"

"I don't know." I stare at him, and he stares at me.

It's not like we're friends, Leo thinks, and my stomach drops. It's exactly what I was afraid of. Him saying that we're not friends anymore. I feel like I'm falling, and this time it's not a memory. It's the feeling of loss. Of sadness plummeting me.

But Leo is still speaking, and I need to hear what he's saying.

"It's not like we're just friends, you know? Your dad, Tūtū, but especially you—you're part of my 'ohana. And I don't want to lose that. Ever."

206

Twenty-Four

TŪTŪ SAYS THAT SOMETIMES THE best thing that can happen to a garden is a storm. Yes, there's a mess to clean up afterward. Leaves to rake, ʻauwai to clear, mud to sweep. But then the trees are a little lighter. The air is fresher. Everyone breathes easier.

That's what it feels like after Leo and I finally talk. Things aren't suddenly perfect. I still feel tender, and he does, too. But it feels easier between us. When he washes the dishes, I dry and put them away. When I say I need to practice my ʻōlelo, he grabs his textbook and reads along. I tell him about Denny and Titus becoming friends.

"Never saw that coming," he says. Then he tells me a little more about the aftermath of the fight between Denny

207

and Brandon. "They're still not talking to each other. It's been weird."

"I thought maybe something might have changed."

"I don't know how it could."

I want to tell Leo that there's always hope. That maybe the talk Titus and I had with Denny today will set something new in motion tomorrow. Two friends like Denny and Brandon can't stay mad at each other forever, can they? "They were always two peas in a pod, right?"

"Not really," he says. "They're kind of opposites."

"Like us?"

"Nah, they're nothing like us."

I smile. It feels good to hear Leo think of us as, well, an us.

Before she goes to bed, Auntie Nina comes into the office to say goodnight. "We're going out to Ka'ena tomorrow, Clara. You like come?"

Dad's birthday tomorrow, Leo thinks.

So that's why Leo was thinking about this hike in study hall yesterday. I don't want to intrude on what is special for him and his mom.

"No pressure," Auntie Nina says, sensing my hesitation. "If you want me go drop you at the hospital, or if you like hang here, that's okay."

I glance at Leo. *Good if Clara is with us*, he thinks.

"I'd love to come along," I say.

"Get to sleep soon, then," she says. "Want to finish the hike before the sun is too high." She blows us each a kiss good night.

"I'm glad you called us today," he says after his mom leaves the room. "When you needed help."

"Who else would I have called?"

"Pua." *You and her are tight now.*

"I wish."

She does wish she called Pua!?

"I'm glad I called *you*," I clarify. "I wish Pua and I were still tight. I kind of messed things up with her yesterday."

"Her, too? What's with you and Friday?" *And I thought I was having a rough week.*

"I got caught up trying to help Ollie, and I didn't listen to what Pua was trying to tell me. I thought things would be all right. But when I texted her today, she never responded. I think I may have really hurt her feelings, and I don't know how to fix it."

"How did you fix things with me?" Leo smirks. He's teasing me but he's also serious.

"Read your mind," I tease back. Except I'm serious, too.

"You know, Pua, Michelle, and I were at Kaluanui

Stream this morning. The reception wasn't great. Try to text her again. You could even invite her on the hike tomorrow."

"But it's your dad's birthday tomorrow."

"You remembered!"

"I didn't remember on my own," I admit.

"That's okay." *Mom must have told her.* "But for real, the more the merrier."

I take a deep breath and then I text Pua. It's a long message. I tell her about Tūtū being in the hospital, how I'm staying at Leo's and can't have her over like I initially offered. But then I invite her to come hiking and explain that I'd like a chance to talk. Finally, I tell her that I'm sorry for how things went down with Titus and I hope she'll forgive me.

I know she ignored my text earlier today, but that one didn't tell her how I felt. Maybe this one will allow her to understand. If nothing else, I feel better for having apologized. A few minutes later I get this message: *I'll see you at Ka'ena.* That's all. Nothing more.

"What if she gets there and doesn't want to talk to me?" I ask Leo.

"Use your mind reading magic," he jokes. "I'm sure that will solve everything."

❋ ❋ ❋

Tūtū's storm comes that night. Rain pelts the windows and gathers in puddles along the edge of the house. In the morning, the swell has brought major wave action to North Shore. We watch the whitewater churn at the edge of the reef as we drive past Dillingham Airfield. Above, several adventurous skydivers steer themselves across the sky, their parachutes pops of color—red, orange, yellow, pink.

The Waiʻanae Mountain Range rises to our left. When the paved road ends, Auntie Nina parks the car in the dirt next to a huge red boulder. A handful of other cars are here already, and it's not even nine a.m. I look for Pua but don't see her. What if she ends up bailing?

Auntie Nina stuffs a windbreaker and sun hat into her backpack, then checks and rechecks where we placed our water bottles. Leo tosses me a spare sweatshirt. The hike is fully exposed to the sun, but the point can get windy and chilly, so it's good to be ready for anything. Just as I finish smoothing sunscreen onto my face, Leo whispers, "Pua's here. With her mom."

When I turn around, I spot a slender woman with a broad-brimmed hat waving at us. A step behind her is Pua. But before I have a chance to say anything, Auntie Nina calls out. "Chey? Cheyenne Shimibukuro?"

"Nina! I can't believe it."

"I never see you for a long time."

"Leo didn't say you were his mom," Auntie Chey says with a laugh. "All morning the kids worked on that science project, and I never even realized." She and Auntie Nina hug. They're chattering so fast that none of us have a chance to ask *how* they know each other.

Leo doesn't miss a beat, though. He gives Pua a megawatt smile. "And look who else is here." He presses his hands to his face as if my presence is a total surprise.

"Hi, Pua," I say.

She offers a tight smile.

A guy, maybe fourteen, steps out of the car. "Hey. I'm Ikaika. Pua's brother."

"I'm Leo, and this is Clara." Leo practically sings my name. He is acting so over the top. *Gotta make sure Pua stays. Gotta get her and Clara to talk.*

"So you're my sister's friends from school?" . . . *like drama class? . . . here to see some whales . . .*

Ikaika's thoughts come in snippets. I can't seem to hear him fully even though he's standing right in front of me.

"Great school friends!" Leo pumps his fist in the air.

. . . *this guy . . . kinda intense . . .*

"Let's all hike together!" Leo does that huge smile again.

212

He's going to scare them away. He might scare me away! "Hiking buddies!"

But instead of running, Pua is giggling. She catches my eye, and I start laughing, too.

"What is this character you're playing?" she asks Leo.

"I'm not playing a character." *Wasn't I just being super welcoming?*

"Leo thinks he's welcoming you," I say to Ikaika.

. . . sixth graders are so . . . but kind of funny . . .

I wonder why Ikaika's thoughts tune in and out. If maybe it's because he's in ninth grade, just old enough to be at the edge of my abilities. I wonder how my gift will shift as I get older. It's the first time I've thought about the future of my clairboyance.

The aunties, on the other hand, are thinking about the past. "We weren't much older than the kids when we met," Auntie Chey says.

"Intermediate school," Auntie Nina replies, shaking her head. "I was so awkward then."

"You and me both." They laugh. Then Auntie Chey smiles at me. "You must be Clara." I nod, feeling a little shy.

Auntie Nina introduces herself to Pua and Ikaika, and then urges us to hele before the sun gets any higher in the sky.

213

The main trail is wide and flat, made for four-wheelers to off-road. A narrow coastal trail runs closer to the ocean, and it's fun to see all the sandy inlets, but I know Leo and his mom's routine. Hike out on the main trail fast, and then take their time with the coastal trail on the return.

"Now, do I know your husband?" Auntie Nina asks Auntie Chey.

"Robert Higa. You recognize the name? His dad ran the restaurant."

"At the end of Hale'iwa? Where all those food trucks park now?"

"That's the one!" Auntie Chey smiles big. "And what's your husband's name?"

"William. His name was Will Kapena."

The word *was* hovers in the air. There's a silence. And then Auntie Chey says softly, "I remember him. Sweet guy. I was sorry when I heard he'd passed." Her hand grazes Auntie Nina's elbow. It's the smallest touch, but it makes Auntie Nina smile a little.

I glance at Leo. He's caught the moment between the aunties, and it makes him feel both sad and happy. *Nice when someone remembers Dad*, he thinks, before turning his attention to a pair of surfers crossing the sand dunes barefoot. Their shortboards are tucked beneath their arms.

Dad would have stopped to talk story with those guys, and Mom would have teased him to hurry up because it's hot already.

Ikaika is watching the surfers, too, but his thoughts are filled with questions: *How do they even paddle into . . . and across the reef . . . if there are sharks? . . .*

As we pass the surfers, I turn to Pua. "Maybe we can talk?" I slow my pace. She slows hers in response.

. . . they doing? . . . Ikaika stops to wait for us.

"Go ahead, Ikaika." Pua makes a shooing motion with her hands. "We're talking."

"Ooh, hot goss?" Ikaika leans toward us, as if he wants to listen in. *All the things my sister doesn't want Mom to know. . . .*

Pua rolls her eyes. "It's not hot goss. It's girl stuff."

. . . And I'm out! . . . Ikaika jogs to catch up with Leo. "So are you a Mariners fan?"

Leo touches his cap and smiles. "My dad took me to a game at Safeco Field once."

"Safeco, eh? Using the old name. That's cool."

The boys take off, talking about team stats and next season's potential trades.

I turn back to Pua. "Thanks for coming. It means a lot."

"Mom was pretty excited when I said you invited us.

She hasn't hiked here since we moved back."

"And were you excited?"

"I wanted to hear you out." She matches her stride to mine. Our backpacks jostle in time. It's nice to be in tune with someone.

"I'm really sorry about Friday," I say. I keep my eyes on the ground. It's easier apologizing if you have something to look at. "I totally ignored you, even when you were trying to talk to me."

"I was talking out loud."

"You were. You didn't even make me read your mind." I peek up at her, and I'm relieved that she's smiling.

"I was upset," she admits. "But when I read your big text, I thought, I better accept Clara's apology. We only have eight weeks left to hang out."

"One week."

"One week what?"

"One week left. My dad is moving me at the end of this week."

"What? He said Christmas. He can't change that!" Pua stops in her tracks. "I mean, is this what you want?"

I bury my hands in my face. "I don't know. No. I used to, but—"

At that precise moment, a shadow falls across us. I

sense, before I even look skyward, what I'll see.

"It's that bird again," Pua exclaims with wonder. She's shading her eyes to block the sun.

For a second, I think it can't be real. It must be a Laysan albatross or another more common bird. But I'd know those deep black wings and forked tail anywhere. The 'iwa doesn't hover over us this time. Instead, it tilts in the wind currents, following the curve of the sea cliffs until it disappears from sight. "Amazing," Pua sighs.

"Amazing," I agree. But what does it mean? Was that 'iwa supposed to be a guide or a thief? A sign to stay, or a signal to steal away?

"You were telling me about the move," Pua says. We match our stride again.

"Yeah, the move." How do I explain my change of heart? "I felt like moving to Arizona was my way out of here, out of being unhappy. But now . . ."

"Now you have Leo as a friend again?"

"It's not just Leo," I say. "Now I have you as a friend, too."

"No matter where you end up, I'll still be your friend." She swings her pack so it lightly bumps mine, and I bump hers back. I feel so lucky to have met Pua. Lucky that she is forgiving and understanding, and that she knows how to wear down anyone's defenses. Even mine!

Twenty-Five

PUA AND I SPEND THE next half hour talking about our group projects. Apparently, Michelle adored Auntie Chey because she knew so much history about the stream. "She was nicer to me after that," Pua says. "We actually had a great morning together."

"Let's see if it lasts."

"It's funny," Pua muses. "I think I get Michelle a little more. I used to say I was from Seattle because I had grown up there. But when Michelle talks about being from here, it means something different. Something deeper. It's not only where she lives or was born, or even where her parents were born. It's about actually being from this land." Pua pauses to take a swig from her water bottle. "I mean, you must feel the same way."

218

I use my water bottle as an excuse to buy myself time to think about what Pua is saying. I don't actually think I've felt like I'm from this land. Or at least I didn't know enough to understand that feeling. But now . . . "I think I'm beginning to understand what it means to say I'm from here," I tell Pua. "And I also think I've got a lot more to learn."

Soon enough we pass between these huge boulders and come to a tall fence that crosses the trail and runs all the way to the ocean. The boys are waiting for us by the gate.

"What's this for?" Pua asks.

"It's for the bird sanctuary," I explain. "It keeps out predators like mongoose and rats."

"Clara knows so much about birds," Leo says. *Tell them what season it is. I never remember.*

"Nest building season starts soon," I say. "On the ground you can look for mōlī. Laysan albatross. You might even see one trying to take off. They're super awkward on land. They sort of half leap, half throw themselves into the wind."

"Isn't this where souls leap into the afterlife?" Ikaika asks.

"It's called a leina-a-ka-'uhane," Leo says. "You can think of it as afterlife. Or you can think of it as the place where our spirits, after we die, are reunited with our family and friends." *It's why Mom and I come here for Dad's birthday.*

"I feel like every place on Oʻahu has some special history," Pua says.

"Every place has stories," I say. "Some are recorded to share, and some are private, passed down among families."

"And some are happening to us right now," Leo adds. *That's what my dad used to say.*

As we hike, Pua and the guys keep scanning the ground for mōlī. I keep looking into the sky, wondering if the ʻiwa will return and give me clearer guidance.

Farther below us the ocean heaves against the black shelves of reef. The feeling I get out here is like none other. The land is wild and hallowed at once. As we get closer to the point, Leo catches up to Auntie Nina, and Auntie Chey and Ikaika drop behind, studying the dunes. At this distance, I can't hear any of Leo's or Ikaika's thoughts, and I'm glad. In a place like this they should have privacy, their emotions safe from prying ears like mine.

At the point, we break out our snacks and trail mix. We search for monk seals among the rocks and whales arriving early for the winter season. Leo points out a spout of water to Ikaika and Pua, but neither he nor I can decide if it was actually a whale or just the wind blowing across the surface of the ocean.

Auntie Chey insists on taking photos of us four kids

with the ocean behind us. Then she offers to take a picture of Auntie Nina and Leo. They pose next to each other, and Leo puts his arm around his mom's shoulders. They smile in the first picture and then, without talking about it, they both get serious for the second. "Clara, come join us," Auntie Nina beckons, but I hesitate. Does Leo want me there?

I shouldn't have been nervous. Leo motions me over. *Like in the old days*, he thinks as he slings his arm around my shoulders.

On the way back we explore one of the old World War II bunkers and peek at the tide pools. As we reach the end of the hike, Leo joins his mom and Auntie Chey to hear a story about their high school days. *Dad would have liked this*, I overhear him thinking.

I take Ikaika and Pua down to a little beach where we can sit on the soft sand. We take our shoes off and let our toes burrow into the warmth.

. . . how does Leo hike this in flip-flops? . . .

"Slippers," I say, without thinking.

"Huh?"

"Oh, nothing. I was thinking that here we call flip-flops slippers."

Ikaika laughs. "It's like you read my mind."

221

"If only you knew," Pua mumbles.

Ikaika points to a couple of surfers, way out past the reef. Maybe they're the same guys we saw earlier. "Is this a popular break?"

"It's not crowded, if that's what you mean," I say. "But on a day like this, you've got to know what you're doing."

The surfers are waiting. They appear perfectly still, seated on their shortboards, but underneath the water their feet are kicking and churning. They watch the horizon. And then, before we can see what's tipped them off, they start paddling for shore. Soon enough, a wave rises behind them. Without looking over his shoulder, one goes for it— paddling as hard as he can. In an instant, he stands and sweeps down the face before cutting up again. The reef is gnarly here, not something a surfer wants to be dropped on by a ten-foot wall of water.

"He didn't even look behind them," Ikaika marvels.

"Why would they look behind?" I ask, confused.

"To see where the wave is."

"They don't need to look. They know."

"But how?"

"Magic," Pua says sleepily. She's lying on her back, eyes closed.

"For real. How do they know, Clara?"

I think about it, and then I instruct Ikaika, "Close your eyes." He closes them. "Tell me when the next wave is closing out."

"How do I do that?" . . . *some kind of trick?* . . .

This inlet has a million sounds. Wind, water rushing up the sand, kids yelling on the trail behind us, people laughing. An ATV rumbling in the distance. But you can always hear the waves. The way they suck back a little, get quiet as they build. How they heave and burst. It's even louder when you're in the water.

"Now!" Ikaika says, and he opens his eyes in time to see the second surfer get eaten by whitewash. "That's a good trick."

"No trick. Comes from knowing the water. When you're out there, it's not only the sound. You can feel it, too." The tilt of the wave, how it moves under you. Where it starts to flatten. When it kicks and sprays.

I'm not even much of a surfer and I know all this. I've been taught it. By Dad, Tūtū, Leo, the ocean itself.

I don't want to leave this place. It's not just all the ways I know it, am familiar. It's also everything I have to learn. Like all the stories about ʻiwa, or Keaʻau, or the shrimp who live in the Kaluanui Stream.

Arizona seems super cool with its cactus and canyons

and deserts. One day I might be lucky enough to be a guest there, learn its landscapes. But it will never be home.

How am I going to tell Dad all this? I've spent almost three months convincing him to let me move. He even went and found a permanent job in Phoenix. And now I want to take it all back. Will he be mad at me? Disappointed? And what will happen between him and Tūtū? What if he thinks she put me up to it, and they never speak again?

Next to me Ikaika sighs. . . . *very major . . . can't believe that I . . . life-changing . . .*

"What's going on over there?" I ask.

"I've had an epiphany." . . . *totally essential . . . tell Mom and Dad . . .*

"Should I be worried? Are you okay?"

"Everything is clear now." Ikaika sighs again. "I've gotta learn how to surf."

Twenty-Six

LATE IN THE AFTERNOON, AUNTIE Nina picks up Dad from the airport. I stay back with Leo. I know I should go, be there to greet Dad, but I'm nervous. What am I going to say when I see him? How am I going to talk to him about this move?

When he and Auntie Nina show up at the house, I don't have to feel shy. "You've grown!" Dad says, lifting me into the air. I squeeze him as hard as I can. It feels great to be wrapped in a huge hug. Our big convo can wait.

"Leo, howzit?" He offers Leo his hand and they do some complicated handshake. At the end, Dad pulls Leo in for a hug. "Missed you, too."

"How's Tūtū?" Leo asks.

"They're going to keep her one more night for obser-vation, but she's breathing without oxygen now. We'll go to the hospital after your mom drops us at home."

There's that word: *home.* Dad thinks of this as home, too. But he's been determined to make things work in Ari-zona. Has that been all my doing?

"You sure you can't stay for dinner?" Leo asks. "Mom can pick up food."

"Oh, can I?" Auntie Nina rests her hands on her hips.

Dad laughs. "I'll cook for you folks later this week."

But it's Dad's birthday today.

"Tūtū will want to celebrate Uncle's birthday, too," I say.

Dad gives me a funny look—surprised and sad and probing. He turns to Leo. "I need time for marinate your dad's favorite ribs. Wouldn't be right to eat any kine food."

As long as we get to hang out before you go. And before Clara goes, too.

I give Leo a quick hug before I hop in the car with Dad and Auntie Nina, who's dropping us off at home. "See you tomorrow," Leo says. *Can't believe it'll be our last week in school together.*

Not if I have anything to say about it, I want to say. "Talk to you on the bus?"

"Yeah." He smiles. "Talk to you on the bus."

In the car I finally have a chance to study Dad. He looks different. Tired. Purple half-moons under his eyes. His hair has grown shaggy. He needs a day at the beach or in the loʻi. He needs some time on island.

As he gazes out the window, he sighs. I can tell that the drive brings back a lot of memories. This is his old stomping grounds. But I can't dip into those memories without something that belongs to him, and there's nothing of Dad's in Auntie Nina's car. No tie. No sunglasses. Only the shirt he's wearing. It's pretty faded but I can still make out the letters: HECO. Hawaiian Electric Company. I reach between the front seats and grab a corner of his shirt. He glances at me, mystified, then smiles. "You used to do that when you were little. Hold on to my shirt like this." His attention returns to the window. I close my eyes and wait for a memory to surface. This time I don't fall. This time the visions come in fragments.

My dad as a boy in front of a portable hibachi grill, his feet dug into sand. . . . Tūtū and Papa bracing a lime tree when it's still a sapling. . . . Uncle Will and Dad with their fishing tackle in the back of a truck . . . My mom at thirteen, long hair swirling around her waist.

Even if the memories are fragmented, I feel the sweetness in them. How coming back here makes Dad feel happier, more relaxed, more like himself. And if he feels happier, then I know he can be convinced to let me stay here, to even come back himself.

But I don't want to be the one to tell him the plan has changed. Not after all the work he went through to make Arizona happen. Auntie Nina wouldn't be the one to do that either. Tūtū, however . . .

When Auntie Nina drops us off at the house, I make a point to grab the 'umeke I carved. I tuck the wooden bowl in my schoolbag and climb into Tūtū's truck.

Now it's my turn to spend a car ride lost in my thoughts. But I have to plan things carefully. I want Tūtū to be able to speak her mind with Dad. To tell him how important it is for us to stay here. For me to stay here. And then I need Dad not to argue with her. That's where the 'umeke comes into play. It will help him listen to her, hear her. It will keep her from losing her temper with him. With the 'umeke in my hands, I can get Tūtū to convince Dad to move home. Then we'll all be happier.

At the hospital, Tūtū is napping. She doesn't have an oxygen mask covering her face anymore. She's still wearing a hospital gown, though, and her arms are bare. Their fleshy folds remind me of grooves in tree bark. It's a beautiful sight to me.

Tūtū opens her eyes and smiles. "There's my Shrub!" Then she sees Dad. Her tone turns serious. "Koalani." Yet she still opens her arms to him.

"Mom, you looking too good to be in this place." He holds her close and kisses her cheek.

"Did you hear the rain last night?" I pull a chair up to the hospital bed and rest my backpack on my feet. "The storm you predicted definitely hit."

"I told you, Shrub." She puts her fingers to her temples, like I taught her to do, and I wiggle my fingers like a gigantic octopus. She laughs.

"I don't get it," Dad says, but he's smiling.

I let her and Dad talk about ordinary things: how his flight was, what food they've been serving her in the hospital. "They got me eating a low-sodium diet," she tells him, and makes a face. "Ah, but too much about me. You look tired."

"Worried about you is all." He takes her hand in his. "Wish I could have gotten a flight here sooner."

"It's hard living so far apart," I say. I unzip the top of my backpack. *Get ready, little 'umeke*, I think.

"Hard, hard," Tūtū says in a singsong voice. "But you here now. That's what matters."

Since when has Tūtū been so easygoing? And why is Dad nodding along?

I need to give them another nudge. "Beautiful hike today at Kaʻena. Brought back so many memories."

"The drive to see you did, too." Dad kisses Tūtū's hand.

Okay, now we're getting somewhere. Tūtū is definitely going to build off that, tell Dad how he could live those good times again.

"Hard, some of those memories," Tūtū says. "That Leo, he went break my heart. Couldn't even come inside the hospital to see Tūtū."

No! This is not the direction I want to go in! Dad has to remember why he loves this place, not the painful parts. And I already feel bad about Leo thinking I didn't want him in here. Now I'm learning that I disappointed Tūtū, too?

I have to redirect them. I pull the ʻumeke from my backpack. "I made this for you both." I hold it out. "It's so you can listen to what each other has to say. Really hear one another."

"I think I know where you got that from." Tūtū caresses the ʻumeke tenderly.

"Was it the book Steph sent you?" Dad asks.

"The pattern was from the book but the idea from Tūtū." I place the ʻumeke in Dad's hands, and he cradles it. I've taken fine-grit sandpaper to the outside to make it smooth and polished it with coconut oil so it gleams. "This is really beautiful." He hands it to Tūtū to study.

"So precious. I going keep it right next to the other," she says. "I ready listen now. What you like tell me, son?"

"I'd like to wait until you're home to have big talks."

"Oh, big talks. Well, I'll be ready then. We'll talk about Christmas and the wedding and get things squared."

"Tell her, Dad." I squeeze my hands together in anticipation. She's going to set him right in three . . . two . . . one . . .

He takes a deep breath. "I plan to bring Clara back with me next week. I want you to come, too. Steph and I want to take care of you."

I wait for Tūtū to burst with emotion—tears or wailing or anything. When that doesn't happen, I expect her to scold Dad, to stay steady if imperious. And when *that* doesn't happen, I wait for her voice to get low, like it does when she's very disappointed in someone. But all I get is . . . silence. She says nothing. For the first time in my life, I wish I could read Tūtū's thoughts.

"I didn't put any poi in it," I say. "So you can say anything."

"What you want me for say?" Tūtū's voice is small. "This decision leaves me with no words."

"Mom—" Dad starts, but he stops. He has no words either.

After a long pause, she says, "Perhaps you should go."

I look from one to the other. I don't understand. These past few months they've bickered and argued and gone back and forth. But now, faced with Dad's decision, they say nothing?

"Come give Tūtū a hug," she says to me. I press my ear to Tūtū's chest and listen to her steady heartbeat, the whirs and whispers of her lungs. When I pull away, she looks at me gently. "I going support you, whatever you decide. But this your decision for voice." She kisses me on the forehead.

Dad is silent on the way to the parking lot, silent as he navigates the car past the shrimp trucks. It's only when we've reached home that he lets out a heavy sigh, the kind that whooshes dust off the dashboard. "I mean, moving you to Arizona is the thing to do, right?"

I don't know how to answer. I was certain that getting Tūtū and Dad to listen to one another would be our way forward. Dad would speak, then Tūtū would disagree, then he would hear her. And just like that, we'd all stay here. But that's not what happened. *This your decision for voice*, Tūtū said.

I wanted them to listen to each other, but I failed to realize that you can only hear someone if they're willing to speak.

Twenty-Seven

THE NEXT DAY IN HOMEROOM I keep my eyes on the clock, counting the minutes. Denny and Brandon are in with Kumu Apo, and I'm hoping they can hear each other out. Otherwise, it might be my last chance to help them repair their friendship. As soon as class is over, I plan on rushing to the office so I can meet up with Denny. I want to hear how it went.

When class is almost over, I pack my gel pens, get ready to move. "Clara," Kumu Whitman says as the bell rings. "Can you stay after, please?"

Not now! I glance at the classroom door as my class-mates stream into the hall. I don't have time for this. But I know Kumu Whitman would only ask me to stay if it was something important. "What is it, Kumu?"

"How are you doing?" he asks. "You seem a little . . . distracted."

I am distracted! "I told Denny I'd meet him." I inch toward the door.

"Isn't he in Kumu Apo's office with Brandon?"

I nod.

"I didn't know you and Denny were friends."

"We're not. Or, I mean . . ." I think about it. We weren't friends a week ago. I wasn't friends with Pua a week ago. Or Titus. I had barely said more than a few sentences to Nalu or Ollie. Yet in the last week my clairboyance has made me bold in ways I've never been before. I've made big mistakes, like egging Brandon and Denny into a fight. But I've also made some good decisions. Like making things right with Leo.

"Earth to Clara." Kumu Whitman smiles at me gently. "This is what I'm talking about. You keep traveling into outer space. I don't mind. I just want to be sure you're okay. I was really surprised when Kumu Apo told me you'd gotten in trouble on the bus."

"Ugh, that." I cover my eyes with my hand. I still feel embarrassed about throwing Leo's hat out the window, even if he and I have made up. "Sometimes I do stuff and I don't think through what could happen."

"I've been there. Sometimes I think the best super-power would be the ability to see the consequences of our decisions ahead of time."

"Now that's the gift I should have asked for."

"Gift?" Kumu Whitman tilts his head in confusion.

"I mean, that would be such a gift to have."

"And yet, it's kind of amazing the unexpected outcomes along the way." He pats his yellow school tie.

I glance at the clock on the wall. I need to get going if I want to catch Denny, but I also want to ask Kumu Whitman about his school tie and the memory I glimpsed. I decide to go for it. "What is it about that tie that makes it so special?"

"I've told the class before. It helps me remember why I became a teacher."

"But it seems like you didn't like your school."

"Did I admit to that?"

"Umm, you mentioned the debate team?"

"Wow, when did I do that?" Kumu Whitman shakes his head, confused. "I mean, yeah, it's what you said. I tried out for debate. Mathletes. Sports teams. None of the other boys wanted me. Teachers didn't make it any easier. You know why I select your project groups? Because I never want anyone to be left out. It's a rotten feeling. And it happens to the same kids over and over." He picks up the tie and unfolds it so the satin finish catches the light. "Finally, I told my mum how bad it was, and she let me change schools."

"Then why do you keep that school tie, if it's the school you left?"

"Back then, I spent a lot of time staring out of classroom windows. I started to keep track of what I observed. Plants, animals, changes in the seasons. It's what made me want to study science and become the kind of teacher I wished I had. My secondary school was rotten. But weirdly, it set me on the right path. That, and my mum. She got me out of there and into a school where I was happy." He sets the tie down and smiles at me. "That was more than you probably wanted to know."

"It was pretty interesting, actually."

"I don't know about that." Kumu Whitman smiles. "But hey, you better get going if you want to catch Denny."

I glance at the clock. "You're right!" At the classroom door I pause and look back. "You're a good teacher, Whitty."

"Wha—?" Kumu Whitman exclaims, but I'm already dashing out the room and down the hall, headed for the main office.

I arrive there as Denny and Brandon are stepping into the hall. I don't want to look like I'm spying on them, so I grab a flyer from the announcement board and pretend to read it. With so many kids passing between class periods, it's hard to pick one thought out from another, but I search for Denny's and Brandon's voices. I trace my finger on the flyer, pretend to draw a flower. Anything to focus me.

"Hey, Clara!" Denny is right behind me!

I spin around, still clinging to the flyer, as if it's some kind of invisibility shield. "What are you two doing here?" I say, feigning surprise.

"Just talking story," Denny says. "I heard Waimea was going off yesterday."

"I didn't get to see it. I was at Leo's."

"Next time we hang out we'll have to go down to the bay."

"Next time?" Brandon says. "Why hang out with Mousey if you're not forced to?"

I wince. This is why I didn't want to be seen.

"Dude." Denny elbows him. *Don't be a jerk. Not right after we got out of that session.* "Clara's cool. And she's got secret powers."

"What?" I gasp. Did Denny somehow find out?

"Don't be random," Brandon says.

"She can hear people's thoughts," Denny says, his voice low and serious. "I witnessed it at the heiau by her house."

I exhale a sigh of relief. He's talking about the voices on

the wind. "Careful, Brandon," I say, playing along. "Or I'll read your mind."

"Whatever," Brandon grumbles. *Denny's joking, right? Clara can't really hear what I'm thinking, can she?*

I can't believe Brandon is believing this, even a little. "You're wondering if I can hear your thoughts."

"That's not true." *How did she do that?*

"You're wondering how I did that."

"Okay, this is weird."

Denny starts cracking up. "We gotta get to class," he says to Brandon. "Catch you later."

"Later, freaks," Brandon says. But as he walks away, I hear, *Maybe I shouldn't mess with Clara anymore.*

"You played that so well," Denny says when Brandon's gone.

"I may have actually scared him." I chuckle. "You and him seem cool again."

"You know, I thought about what you said at the heiau on Saturday. How if you were a kahuna, you'd just listen. And, I don't know, I wanted to yell at Brandon and stuff. But instead, I waited a beat and heard him out, and . . ." Denny trails off. "It wasn't cool how Brandon handled being jealous, but it was worse that I hit him."

I'm floored. I *helped* Denny. Not by using my powers or in any of the ways I set out to, but by talking to him. Getting to know him. Being . . . a friend. I'm proud of myself. I fixed something. And I'm happy for Denny and Brandon.

"What happens now?"

"We have a bunch of school service hours coming. But we're allowed on the bus again."

"So you're back to being besties?"

"We'll see. We're cool with each other, but I don't know if he's my crew anymore."

I hold open the door to Kumu Whitman's classroom. "If Brandon's not your crew, then who's—"

"Ho, cuz!" Denny says as soon as he sees Titus. They high-five before Denny heads to his desk.

I grab the seat next to Titus. "So you *are* entering Anywhere in the Worlds," he says.

"Huh?"

He points to the flyer still in my hand. I almost forgot about my invisibility shield.

"Ollie and I are working on Frodo's shire. Nalu is re-creating Narnia. What are you going to do?"

"I don't think I'm doing anything."

"You should. You're a great artist. I've seen your sketches."

"How?"

"You're always drawing cool stuff on your planner and in the margins of your notes."

"I didn't think anyone noticed."

Sometimes Clara thinks she's invisible. "Anyway, you should do the contest. I hear they're getting a real artist to judge. There's going to be a fancy breakfast for everyone who enters. And a chance to hang out with everyone else who entered." Titus pauses like he wants to say more. *Maybe Clara knows if Pua is going to submit something?*

"You talked me into it," I say. "And I'll tell Pua to enter, too."

Twenty-Eight

I FINISH EARLY WITH MY school service in the library, so I make it out to the benches for the last half of the lunch period. I'm surprised to find Denny there, sitting with Titus and Pua and Nalu, all of them chatting away about the Anywhere in the Worlds contest. "Library duty go okay?" Pua asks.

"Pretty easy, actually." I unpack the tuna sandwich Dad made for me while everyone goes back to chatting

I look over at Titus, Pua, Denny, Ollie, and Nalu deep in discussion. So much of getting to know someone is talking with them, listening. I think of Saturday with Titus and Denny. How fun it ended up being. And hiking with Leo and Pua. How today, in class, I felt close to everyone in a new way. If I can't convince Dad to stay, I want to enjoy the time I have left with them.

I sneak my phone out of my backpack and text Tūtū with an idea. She should be home from the hospital by now. A few minutes later, my phone vibrates. Tūtū tells me that my plan is a go—but also to put my phone away.

"Hey," I call across the table to everyone. "Would you want to come over on Saturday? It would be a work day in Tūtū's loʻi but you could take kalo home."

"No fair!" Nalu says. "I'm on Maui then."

"I'll text you photos," Titus says. "That place is awesome. Ask Denny."

"Totally awesome," Denny agrees.

What about Hoku and Jade? Ollie thinks. *I'm still supposed to hang out with them.*

"I didn't forget about Hoku and Jade," I tell him. "I figure that if it's okay with you, we can invite them over, too. Then we can all hang out together and have fun."

"What if Hoku doesn't like getting dirty or doesn't want to spend her Saturday harvesting taro?"

"Something tells me Hoku is up for anything. You want me to ask her now?"

"Um . . ." Ollie hesitates. It doesn't take clairboyance to see that he's super nervous. But there's a soft whispered thought I pick up. *I want to ask her myself.*

"Or I don't have to do the asking. I can just walk over with you," I suggest. Ollie nods.

When Jade and Hoku see us coming their way, they whisper something to each other. Even I feel nervous, and I'm not the one with the crush. At their table, I give Ollie a little wave. And then I keep walking. I have one more invitation to extend.

As I near the banyan tree I feel nervous. Will Brandon make fun of me? Will Michelle tell me to go away? Will Leo talk to me now that we're at school and in front of other people?

I needn't have worried. Michelle ignores me, which isn't a bad thing, and Brandon offers me a nod of acknowledgment. No nicknames. No teasing. The extent of Brandon's thoughts are this: *Oh, one of Denny's friends.*

Leo, for his part, gives me a big smile. "I'm headed to check in with Kumu Whitman. You want to walk over together?"

"Sure." I'm relieved I don't have to talk to him in front of the others. Once we're out of earshot, I say, "I'm having folks over on Saturday for a work party in the loʻi. You want to come? It may be a farewell party, too."

"I'll be there. But I don't like the farewell part."

"Neither do I."

"I thought you wanted to go." *See more of the mainland. Live somewhere new and exciting.*

"All that's changed now. The most exciting place I can think to be is here. I don't know how to explain that to my dad, though. Not even Tūtū could convince him to come back home."

"Maybe he needs to hear it directly from you." *Like how I should have talked directly to Clara instead of giving Michelle a note to deliver.*

"Honestly, writing a note sounds pretty good right now." *How'd Clara know I was thinking about that note? Weird!*

"You didn't need a note to talk to me this weekend."

"I kind of did, actually. I wrote you an apology note on Friday. I just never handed it to you."

"For real?" Leo smiles. "Then write a note to your dad. But think of it as a draft of what you want to tell him." *Like apparently you did with me.*

"And if it doesn't work? If Dad still insists on moving?" I twirl my flyaways in the same way Leo spins his curls when he's stressed. "It's not only about me, you know. I'm worried Tūtū will be left all alone."

"Tūtū will never be all alone. My mom and I will make sure of that." *Tūtū's our tūtū, too.* Leo holds open the door to the science building, and I slip into the hall. It's cool and quiet in here. "You should say what you're thinking," Leo continues. "You can't expect your dad to read your mind."

Ha! If only Leo knew my family's gifts. But Leo's right. Reading my mind is clearly not Dad's gift, so I have to be honest with him. And as long as I'm trying to be honest, I want to tell Leo the truth. He's my best friend, so if Pua knows about my gift, then he should, too.

"There's something else I wanted to talk to you about," I start. But what if he's angry when he finds out I've been reading his mind all this time? I wimp out. "Never mind." I don't want Leo and me to get into a fight right after we've become friends again.

"Come on, tell me." He pauses in front of Kumu Whitman's classroom and leans back against the lockers. "If you're leaving in a week, then you might as well lay all the secrets on me."

He says that now, but once he finds out, then what? I peer down at my shoes before looking up at him again. I don't want to do this, but I know I need to do this. "You're not going to believe what I'm about to tell you. And it might make you mad at me."

"Okaaaaay." *Did she do something to another one of my hats?*

"Your hats are safe!"

Leo glances at me sidelong. *Clara has been in my head so much lately.*

I take a deep breath. "The truth is I can hear what you're thinking." I squeeze shut my eyes, nervous about what will come next.

First there's silence, and then there's . . . laughter?! I open one eye, then the other. Leo's doubled over, he's laughing so hard.

"I'm for real." I take him by the shoulders. "I can hear your thoughts!"

That makes him laugh even harder.

Should I laugh, too, pretend this is all a joke? Should I insist on him believing me? But before I can decide, Leo slings his arm around my neck.

"Clara, I believe you, but," he says, smiling, "you've *always* been able to tell what I'm thinking. You're my best friend, after all."

Twenty-Nine

WHEN I ARRIVE HOME THAT afternoon I find Tūtū seated in a lawn chair beside the loʻi. She's got a bucket of ʻohā beside her, but she isn't replanting. "Gotta take it easy," she tells me. "Doctor's orders. Just like show these babies where they going this weekend."

I wrap my arms around her. She smells like coconut oil and lemon, earth and sun. The rattle is gone from her chest, and she breathes with ease. She says my dad is at the grocery store, and I can tell by the stiffness in her voice that they still haven't addressed the news he dropped yesterday.

I dip my feet into the loʻi. The ʻauwai is filled with cold mountain water. My ankles ache with the chill, but when I burrow my feet into the soft, silty mud, my toes are cozy and warm. "Thanks for letting me invite over a bunch of people on Saturday."

"I'm happy, Shrub. Sounds like we got some good strong workers coming. And maybe some good strong friendships, too." She points to the edge of the loʻi. "Eh, plant a row there for me."

I follow Tūtū's direction and press an ʻohā several inches into the soft earth. I whisper to it to grow strong. I feel close to Hāloa, and I want to see this ʻohā become a makua. To harvest what I've planted here.

The back screen door slaps and Dad appears on the patio, waving. "I'm going to get dinner started," he calls out. Tūtū doesn't look up, but I motion for Dad to come join us. He hesitates before eventually making his way down the hillside.

"I hope you're not pushing yourself," Dad warns.

"Don't worry. I not lifting one finger." Her words are clipped. I can tell she's annoyed at him for fussing over her.

He frowns but doesn't reply. After a minute, he points to some fully grown kalo and asks, "Can I harvest a couple of these to steam tonight?"

Tūtū nods. No words spoken.

I miss when Tūtū and Dad were arguing. At least then they talked to each other.

Eventually we all come in from the lo'i. I swear the leaves bob up and down in relief when we leave, as if even the taro has been waiting to relax after that bout of tense silence. I head to my room for my own little break.

I think about Leo's advice to gather my thoughts in a note. Even if it was hard to write the apology letter to him, it did help. And I did finish it eventually. So, I sit down and try to jot down something for Dad. I want to tell him about Leo and me making up, and about my new friendship with Pua. I want to explain how it feels to be learning the place that we're from. But all my thoughts feel too complicated for words.

So I check out Dad's drawing again. Maybe I can get another read off it, another memory that will help me find better words. I pull the frame from the wall and close my eyes. But this time nothing happens.

When I open my eyes, the whorls and curls and loops are still there. But now they seem familiar. I can't put my finger on it, yet I know I've seen these patterns before. I open the back of the frame and slip out the drawing. On the back, in light pencil, are the words: *our dreaming place*.

Our dreaming place? What's a dreaming place? And how do a bunch of whorls become one?

Which is when it clicks. These loops and scraggly lines

demark an *aspect* of place: elevation! Exactly what Denny and Titus showed me for our science project. Dad's drawing is a topographic map!

But how do I find his dreaming place?

The little icons could be landmarks, I guess. There's a jester hat. Jester? Fool? Jesters hang out in courts. But the nearest basketball or tennis courts are by the ocean, and these lines indicate something more mauka, inland. The happy face isn't any better. Could it represent joy? A smile? An emoji? Did they even have emojis when Dad was a kid?! The other symbols are no easier to understand. A cup or mug. A slipper. An upside-down question mark in the middle of a circle.

The only part of the drawing I can identify is the ʻiwa soaring above everything else, but what does it mean? Is the goal of the map to find a guide, like Kumu Maka did? Or something of our ancestor, the boy thief? Obviously, this "dreaming place" meant enough to Dad for him to draw a map of it. Maybe it will hold the key to making him want to move back home.

As I study the drawing, I realize there's one more icon— one I understand. In the corner, at the lowest elevation, is a triangle over a square. Exactly like what Titus drew on

Saturday to mark the location of our house. This is my starting point. Home!

Dad is out in the front yard, so I run out there to tell him I've figured out his drawing. Or at least part of it. Maybe we can do the rest together. But before I step off the front porch, I hear him on the phone. "I know, babe," he's saying. "Tell me what you think I should do." I stop short. He's talking to Steph. He's asking her for advice. I wish it was me he was talking to. Me who he wanted to problem-solve with.

I withdraw back inside before he notices me. I drop the frame on the everything table. If he's too busy making plans, then I can figure this map out on my own. I tie up my tennis shoes and head out to the road. He doesn't even see me leave.

I know I need to climb in elevation, so I head up the hill. The nearest symbol, the jester hat, looks familiar. The asphalt dead-ends, but there's a gravel driveway heading to the Boy Scout camp. I follow it.

At the Boy Scout camp I stop and stare at the sign. Then it hits me. The icon isn't of a jester's hat. It's a fleur-de-lis. The Boys Scouts' symbol. It's right here, in front of me! I'm on the right track.

I follow the same path that the 'iwa led me down the other evening. The dirt path turns into a paved road, and I keep going. I hold the map out in front of me. It's hard to follow because it doesn't have any trails or streets marked, but I know I need to climb in elevation. If I do that, I can reach the upside-down question mark in the middle of the circle.

I pass a dirt trail off the side of the road and double back. There's a wooden sign with a tiny yellow arrow. Should I take this turn-off, or keep going? The map is no help. Both ways seem to gain elevation.

I remember my conversation with Ikaika on the beach at Ka'ena, and describing to him how surfers use more than one sense to navigate the water. Maybe that's what I need to try now. I close my eyes. Tree branches shake in the breeze. A cool draft of air dries the sweat on my arms. I take a deep breath and smell something medicinal and woodsy. It's coming from the direction of the dirt trail, so I follow it. I can always turn back around if I need to. Up, up, and around a bend. Suddenly I'm surrounded by eucalyptus trees. It's all I can smell! And it dawns on me. That upside-down question mark—it's a nose! And the circle is a face. It's telling me to breathe in, to smell.

I'm confident this is where I'm supposed to be. I jog

down the trail. The earth is covered in leaves, and a thick mesh of branches shade me. The sun is dipping behind the mountains, so I can't stay out here long. But the thrill of figuring out the map, this mystery, keeps drawing me forward.

At first the hiking trail is clearly marked. There's even an arrow with the silhouette of a hiker. But soon enough, a dozen or more hunting trails crisscross the main path, and it's less clear where to go. I look at the drawing for the nearest symbol. It's gotta be a coffee mug or teacup. But it's pretty far away. So I do what Denny taught me and study the elevation lines. It looks like there's a gulley between me and the cup. So I'll need to walk downhill and uphill again before I reach my next marker.

I follow the one path that angles down and sure enough, before long, I'm in a gulley. It's darker here. The hillsides block the ambient light. The trees growing on the hillside seem to tower. I cross a streambed and am swarmed by mosquitos. As soon as I've climbed out of the first gulley, I descend into a second.

Where can the next marker be? Is it possible I took the wrong path? I brainstorm ideas. Mug, as in muggy weather? Cup, as in buttercups? I keep my eyes to the ground, searching for yellow buttercups. And then, without warning, the air around me turns green. I am inside a glowing tunnel, otherworldly and beautiful. On either side and above me are ti leaves, illuminated by the fading daylight. I reach out to run my fingers along the smooth ti leaf and realize I found it. *Tea. Ti.* Dad's love of puns!

Eventually I emerge on a ridge. I pull out my cell phone to text Tūtū or Dad, but I have no reception up here. I should turn back. But I don't want to. I thought that listening was hard to learn how to do properly. But maybe learning to speak, to give voice to what's in your heart, is even harder. Like for poor Ollie, who was so nervous to talk to Hoku. Yet, when he finally got up the bravery, when he spoke to her directly, there was no misunderstanding.

There's a fork in the trail and I have to make a decision. The next marker—the slipper—must be nearby. I look for a stream or running water, something that could be slippery. But it's totally dry up here. No mud even. Flip-flop? Something that can turn upside down? No, Dad never used the word *flip-flop* until he moved to the mainland. So he wouldn't have made a symbol of it either. Sandal? Sandy? No beach near here either.

And then I remember: Dad and Tūtū used to come up here when they were helping with the restoration projects.

Clearing invasive plants. Planting native ones, like sandal-wood.

The sun has disappeared behind the Koʻolaus, though the sky is still filled with ambient light. It will be dark soon. I didn't bring water or a flashlight. I know I need to turn around. That I should probably jog the whole way home. But I don't want to give up. Whatever answer lies in this map, I need to have it.

Sandalwood needs other trees to grow. Host plants. So, I start down one fork in the road, but all I see are bushes. No trees. I backtrack. It has to be the other direction. I take that path and soon enough I'm in a small grove of trees. One of these must be a sandalwood tree, but which one?

Suddenly, I hear clomping and heavy breathing. Some-one is coming up the trail, and they're moving fast.

Thirty

I DASH BEHIND A TREE with bark like woven hair. The trunk isn't thick enough to hide me, but there's a boulder that is. I crouch down and wait. I shouldn't have come up here on my own like I did.

"Clara?" It's Dad's voice. "Clara?"

The footfalls retreat as quickly as they came. I bet he's heading back to the fork in the trail. "I'm here, Dad," I call out.

"Is that you?" He runs into the center of the grove of trees. "Oh, thank goodness." His face is bright red from exertion and his shirt is wet with sweat.

"How'd you know where I was?"

He points to the map in my hand. "You left the frame on the everything table. Tūtū said you had been studying it recently. I realized you probably figured out what it was."

"Topographical map, right?"

"Yeah, but why did you follow it so far? It's practically dark."

"You were talking to Steph, and Tūtū was in her room, and I thought . . ." The truth is, I thought that there'd be some kind of answer up here.

"I brought headlamps, but we should probably head down."

"I want to see this to the end. We must be close." There are only two symbols left: the happy face and the 'iwa.

"We can do it another day."

"Not if I'm moving, we can't."

He hesitates, then seems to relent. "You found the sandalwood, I see." He points to the tree I was hiding near.

I press my nose to the trunk. It smells like any other tree—dusty and woody—but I know that deep inside is an intoxicating scent. Once these hillsides were covered with sandalwood, until it was harvested and shipped away. Here, now, is evidence of Tūtū's care, and Dad's. Of how, once, they used to work together.

"So next up is the smiley face emoji?"

"Just 'Smiley,'" he tells me.

I think back to the vision I had with the map. My parents

in their own world, dreaming of leaving the islands. Then it hits me: "Mom calls you Smiley."

"And what's my real name?"

"Clarence. Clarence Koalani. OMG, Dad!" Of course, Koalani. Koa. As in the koa tree. The smiley face is a code for my dad's namesake.

"That one was your mom's idea."

"I would have never figured that out on my own."

"Well, I wouldn't have been able to get this far with that map. Everything looks different. I wonder how big those koa saplings we planted are by now."

"They should be nearby." I haven't taken two steps before I stumble. The trees have blocked what little light is left.

"Put this on." Dad hands me a headlamp.

As we proceed down the trail, Dad brushes his hands against the trees and leaves and bushes. He even bends down to rub the dirt. "I can't believe the memories that are coming back. I used to come up here all the time."

"With Tūtū or Mom?"

"First with Tūtū, then with your mom. The map you're holding was to your mom's and my special spot. The place where we dreamed about the future."

The trail peters out in the middle of a clearing.

"Something isn't right," Dad says. "This wasn't here before."

We look this way and that. I consult the map. If we backtrack a little, maybe there's an incline we can find to get us to what I think will be a ridge. "I think we have to go back," I say.

"No, no," Dad says. "There's no trail. You have to know where to climb. Like here." Dad points to the smallest break in a dense hillside of bushes. "I'm certain this is it."

Before we know it, we're deep among trees with no clear way out. All the markers have disappeared. I'm worried we're never going to find this dreaming place. And then what? My last hope of staying in Hawai'i will be gone.

"Shoot," Dad says. "I should have brought my compass. Always be prepared! Boy Scout motto."

We start back the way we think we came, but we come out into a clearing neither of us remembers.

"I'm mad at myself," Dad says. "I'm leading us away from home."

"We have your map."

"But we need a landmark to make it make sense," Dad says quietly, almost to himself.

"Are you lost?" I feel nervous. I didn't think Dad could get lost.

"I might be." He looks around, trying to get his bearings.

I know he wants to appear calm for my sake, but I can feel his nervousness.

I close my eyes and think of Kumu Maka's story. Although Kaiona belongs to the Waiʻanae Mountains, I know that there's another ʻiwa here, one that's been visiting me. In my head, I call for its help. When I open my eyes again, Dad is looking up into the sky. "Well, I'll be," he says.

There, high above us, a dark shape is circling, looping, surfing the wind currents. My ʻiwa! It catches a current, kites. I look to see where it's pointing, but that's the edge of the clearing. I'm not about to walk off a cliff!

But I don't think the ʻiwa would mislead me. So I follow it, and once I'm close to the edge, my headlamp sweeps across a steep incline of volcanic rock behind a couple of bushes. I push through the plants. There's no trail here, just crumbly red soil without any purchase. But the ʻiwa is pointing me forward, so I start scrambling up the slope. I slip down, try to crawl up again.

"What are you doing?" Dad calls out. "Be careful."

At the last moment, I nudge my shoes into the dirt to make a toehold and heave myself to the top.

"How are you going to get down? How will I get up to you?" Dad's voice betrays his worry.

"We have our landmark," I call down to him. I recognize

it as soon as I see it. "Push your shoes into the dirt. That's how you can get up."

"I'm not as light as you," Dad pants. He slips twice, but finally he makes it up to me.

"There," I say. Beyond the rich greenery of Waimea Valley, the shops and restaurants of Haleʻiwa, the old mill buildings at Waialua, there is the white shoreline that leads to Kaʻena Point. And to the left of that shore is the Waiʻanae Mountains. The final rays of western light outline Mount Kaʻala. The mountain peak is unmistakable.

"I can't believe it," Dad says. "This is it."

"What is it?"

"This is where your mom and I used to come. There's another way to get here. More direct, through a thicket of koa trees. But you found it all the same." He motions to me. "Come."

I follow him along a ridge and then to a grassy bluff. "Watch your footing," Dad says. "But if you come a little closer and look down, it's worth it." I make my way to the edge of the bluff. Below us is the expansive ocean, the mighty waves that make thick white lines along the reef. I spot Waimea Bay, Sharks Cove. The rock walls of Puʻokinau-o-mahuka heiau, a dark and powerful dash. Someone's swimming pool is a sequin sparkling in the moonlight.

And finally Tūtū's and my loʻi laid out in neat terraces.

"Your mom and I would come up here and see the whole world in front of us," Dad says softly to me. "All the places beyond that ocean we wanted to go."

"So you'd come to this special place to dream about leaving here?"

"I guess you could put it that way."

I can't believe my ears. I worked so hard to reach here, to find a place that would draw Dad back home so I wouldn't have to leave, and all I found is the spot where he used to imagine flying away.

It's so hard finding the right balance between listening and talking, but I know that this moment, right now, is one that requires me to speak. I have to use my voice, like Tūtū and Leo urged me to do.

"All that down there," I say to Dad, "that's our home. Don't you miss it?"

"Every day," he sighs.

"Then why do you want to stay in Phoenix so badly?"

He pats the ground next to him. The earth is still warm from the sun's heat, and the grass is sweet smelling. "You won't believe this," he says, "but a long time ago, when I was young, I asked to be able to hear the voice of anyone who wanted to fly away. I thought it would bring me closer to your mom. And for a while it did. But then she wanted to fly away from me, and I had to face that." I lean my head on his shoulder, and he wraps his arm around me. Over the ocean the moon is rising bright and round. "With my gift, I can hear birds on a branch, and dragonflies perched on a leaf. Pilots and parachuters. Airports are absolute madness for me. I've learned how to deal with those voices. But when things fell apart with Leo and you wanted to fly from this place, that broke my heart. I even started arguing with Tūtū, because she wanted to keep you here."

"I know I wanted to leave before," I say. "But not anymore. Everything's changed. I want to stay here."

He tilts his head and closes his eyes. A position I've struck many times this week. Dad is listening. "I don't hear a single thing with my gift." He opens his eyes and smiles at me. "But I can hear what you're saying loud and clear."

Thirty-One

OVER THE NEXT COUPLE OF days, with Dad's help, I trace a series of patterns. Then I whittle and sand and paint basswood.

On Friday, in lieu of homeroom, nearly twenty of us sixth graders gather in the library to admire the artwork that's been submitted for the Anywhere in the Worlds contest. Pua has made a collage out of photographs of Seattle and Honolulu. She's made one skyline blend into the other. "I wanted something that showed what it's like to move between two worlds," Pua tells me.

Nalu's and Titus's drawings are also amazing. In fact, all the art pieces hanging on the walls of the library are really cool. Some are from books or movies and others from real life. Michelle drew Waikīkī without any hotels. Instead, she painted taro patches, water running from Mānoa and Pālolo valleys to the sea, and four sacred healing stones.

I decided to do something a little more 3D. I cut out poster board and stacked it to mimic Dad's topographical map, painting the whole thing in shades of green and brown. I added blue streams that run through the ravines, and then placed my wooden figurines: a sandal, a disc with a smiley face painted on. And hovering over the highest point, dangling by a piece of fishing wire, is an 'iwa. I used the idea of the comfort bird, carving the 'iwa with little detail and sanding it until its smooth. But the wings are outspread, capturing the sense of flight.

While I get a lot of compliments on my contest entry, it's Leo's drawing that makes me pause. He's rendered the Ka'ena peninsula from the perspective of the ocean, so that the land is reaching out to the viewer. On the shore, so small that you might miss them, are three people. "Leo," I call him over. "Is that you and your parents?"

"That's me and my mom," he says. *Doesn't Clara recognize the third person?*

I look closer. The blue shorts, the tank top. The hair flying everywhere. "Is that . . . me?"

"It's based on the photo Pua's mom took of us last weekend," he says. "Ka'ena may be the place where some souls leap off, but I think it can also be where others come together." *And where they learn to be 'ohana again.*

"I really love it," I say. I don't know how to tell him how it makes me feel—sad and hopeful and cared for, all at once.

"Maybe you'd want to keep it?"

I nod. I don't trust my voice right now.

"You can put it in your room in Arizona. Something to remember me by."

"About Arizona—"

But Kumu Apo is tapping at the microphone. That's okay. I'll have time to tell Leo the news later. He'll get to see his art in my room at Tūtū's. We walk outside to the lānai, where there's a table covered in little muffins and pastries and cups of juice. "There's a special guest judge today," Kumu Apo announces once we're all gathered. "Many of you know them as Kumu Maka, your bus driver. But they're also a working artist, and we are honored to have them select and announce the winners of our Anywhere in the Worlds contest."

Kumu Maka steps onto the little podium. They're wearing their yellow-and-white aloha shirt, the one with the repeated 'iwa pattern. In the breeze the fabric billows slightly, and the birds flap their wings.

"Being an artist can mean recording what is in front

266

of you," Kumu Maka says. "But it also can mean dreaming possibilities far beyond this moment." They pause to let this idea sink in and then they move into naming the contest winners. Pua's collage earns an honorable mention, as does Nalu's drawing of Narnia. Leo comes in second. But the surprise of the morning is that there's a tie for first: Michelle's artwork and mine. "Both of these works were deeply personal," Kumu Maka says, "while also offering a fresh perspective on how to see our world."

Michelle and I go up to the podium to claim our prize—gift certificates to a local bookstore. Afterward, I approach her at the refreshments table. "Your drawing made me see Waikīkī in a whole new way," I tell her.

"Thanks," she says, grabbing a muffin from the table. "Waikīkī is this place with so much history underneath what you see. It shouldn't be defined by hotels and restaurants. It has a different past, and future. Well, you know what I mean."

I do know what she means. And it feels good to hear Michelle include me in that knowing. "Is that why you wanted to study the Ala Wai Canal for the observation journal?"

"Yeah, but I'm glad we did Pua's spot in the end. Her mom showed us these mountain 'ōpae that live there. They were cool." Laughter interrupts our conversation. It's Leo and Denny cracking each other up. Michelle sighs. "Sometimes I wish I knew what boys were thinking."

I nearly spit the juice from my mouth. If only Michelle knew! "I used to wish the same," I manage to say. "But now I think it might be easier to just talk to them."

"Of course you would say that." Michelle rolls her eyes. "Anyway, Leo actually talks to you. I can't seem to hold his attention."

"Maybe it's less about attention and more about conversation?"

"That practically rhymed," she says. "Cute." She grabs another muffin from the table and makes her way over to Leo. "I got this for you," she says.

"Thanks," he replies, before scarfing down the whole thing. *Mmm, blueberry*, he thinks, and I can't help but smile. Classic Leo. He turns back to Denny, and I see this look pass over Michelle's face—half panic, half confusion. "Um, Leo, what's your favorite piece of artwork today?" she asks, and he returns his attention to her. She smiles really big.

"Mrah bwrah mah." The muffin garbles Leo's words. He and Michelle both laugh. It's not quite conversing, but maybe it's a start.

Leo's gift to me has given me an idea. I weave among the groups of kids talking and sipping juice, back to my contest entry. Then I untie the 'iwa from its fishing line. Kumu Maka is at the door of the library, about to depart.

"Kumu," I call out.

They pause and wait for me.

"I want to thank you," I say shyly.

"For what?"

Around us the air buzzes with conversation. People talking, listening, connecting. "Last week, the talk we had helped me a lot." I rest the 'iwa in Kumu Maka's hands.

"Oh, Clara," they marvel. They hold up the bird and turn it this way and that. "To give your art to someone is a big gift. I'm very moved by this."

"Well, the next time someone wrinkles your lucky shirt, you'll still have an 'iwa to guide your way."

Thirty-Two

STEPH JOINS US AT THE end of the week. She and Dad have a lot of important details to work out—jobs and contracts and how, exactly, we're all going to fit into Tūtū's house for the time being. But, to my relief, Steph has decided it's time for her to fly home, too.

On Saturday morning we all awake bright and early. I clean up my bed on the couch, and Dad and Steph neaten my bedroom, where they're staying. We have a lot to prepare for the work party.

Pua's parents arrive bright and early with breakfast enchiladas, and Auntie Nina comes with a crate of papayas. Dad sets chicken long rice to simmering, and Ollie shows up with banana bread he baked himself. All these food scents fill the house, and my stomach growls.

I find Pua's dad and introduce him to Ollie. "Uncle Robert," I say. "Ollie wants to be a chef."

"I love hearing that," Uncle Robert says. "Tell me what got you into cooking?"

I hear Ollie excitedly answering as I head out to the porch. Titus, Denny, Jade, and Pua are already hanging out. Nearby, Tūtū has a huge pot set up on a propane stove. That's where she'll steam the kalo.

Once everyone is present, Tūtū opens us with a pule, prayer. She reminds us that if we mālama the land and tend to Hāloa, then they will always take care of us. After, she pairs those who have harvested kalo before with those who are new to the process. At one point Leo pulls so hard on a stubborn kalo that he ends up landing backward in the mud, on his 'ōkole. But by then our friends have grasped how to twist and lift, and they move methodically to harvest from one lo'i and replant 'ohā in another.

As I work, I catch snippets of conversation. Jade is talking about basketball sneakers with Denny and Titus. Ollie is asking Hoku about her favorite video games. Pua wants to know how Leo learned the 'ukulele, and Ikaika has a million questions for my dad about surfing. Everywhere I look connections are being made, some of them planned for and some of them unexpected.

With so many people working together, we finish harvesting and replanting by noon. The adults are still steaming the corms in batches, but everyone is ready to eat. We pule again, and then we line up to scoop food onto our plates. The adults sit at the table and us kids find spots in the grass to stretch our legs.

"This is living." Denny lies backward, his hand resting on a full stomach.

Next to me, I can hear Leo running Iz lyrics through his head. "You bring your ʻukulele like I told you?" I ask him.

"Better believe it."

Dad gets out his guitar and brings a ʻukulele for Pua to play.

"Oh no," Pua says when I hand it to her.

"Don't worry. My dad will call out the chords for you."

Back in the day, Dad and Leo used to play together all the time. Now they tune up with Pua. They start with "Over the Rainbow," and Pua strums along, hitting most of the chords as Dad calls them to her. I can feel Dad and Leo listening to one another, getting back into the groove. Next, they play "Mahina ʻO Hoku" and "Twinkle, Twinkle, Little Star." Dad does a rendition of "Pūpūkea," and Tūtū dances the hula. Then the adults sing a few more old-time songs that none of the kids know.

Finally, Leo says, "Let's do 'Take Me Home Country Road.'"

"This one I know," Denny says, and Ollie laughs. This one we all know.

Our voices take a minute to find each other, to settle into the rhythm of the melody. But when we hit the chorus our singing echoes across the loʻi and up the mountain, enough to join the birds' songs. *Country road, take me home, to the place I belong.* And at the end we call out the names of all the places that matter to us:

West Mākaha. Mount Kaʻala.

Haleʻiwa. Waimea Bay.

These Koʻolau. My Oʻahu.

AUTHOR'S NOTE

Clairboyance is written in English along with two other languages that are significant to this story and to the islands of Hawaiʻi.

ʻŌlelo Hawaiʻi, or the Hawaiian language, is the indigenous language of Kānaka ʻŌiwi, the Native Hawaiian people. In 1896, the United States territorial government banned ʻōlelo Hawaiʻi from being taught in schools. Many kūpuna have stories of being punished just for speaking Hawaiian with their friends near school grounds. Thankfully, in 1978—with concerted effort from the Hawaiian community—the state legislature added an amendment to the state constitution to promote the study of Hawaiian culture, history, and language in public schools. Today, Kānaka ʻŌiwi and others continue to work to increase the pathways for students of all ages to learn ʻōlelo Hawaiʻi.

What locals call "pidgin," or what is formally known as Hawaiian Creole English, is also an important language in Hawai'i. It developed, like many creole languages, out of a desire to communicate across language barriers. This is what happened on Hawai'i's sugar cane plantations in the mid- to late-1800s as American plantation owners brought in different ethnic groups to work in the cane fields. Without a language in common, those workers pieced together something new—a shared language with its roots in 'ōlelo Hawai'i, Cantonese, Japanese, Portuguese, and English. Today, lots of folks in Hawai'i speak pidgin, and you might hear variations depending on the speaker's age or where on the islands they grew up.

ACKNOWLEDGMENTS

The desk at which I wrote this book faces a window that overlooks a main thoroughfare in our housing complex. From my desk I can hear the voices and laughter of the ʻōpio of Kauʻiokahaloa Nui, and I feel gratitude for them (and their parents!), and the community here.

I am also grateful for Sandra Knobloch, who years ago gave me space to write and a cuddly Mighty to keep on my lap, and a healthy ʻauwai whose sounds were inspiration for this book.

I thank my mentors and friends from *Highlights for Children* and Boyds Mills Press: the values I learned from you still guide my writing and teaching.

I was fortunate to have not one but two phenomenal editors to work with. I thank Claudia Gabel for bringing me the seed of this book and Carolina Ortiz for helping me finish growing it. I'm also grateful for Sophie Schmidt, Jessica Berg, Jessica White, Shasta Clinch, Christine Almeda, Corina Lupp, Sean Cavanagh, Sabrina Abballe, Taylan Salvati, and the entire team at HarperCollins.

And as ever, with thankfulness for my wonderful agent, Markus Hoffmann, whose support buoys me.

I am in debt to Bryan Kamaoli Kuwada and Craig Howes, who offered generous feedback, guidance, and wise counsel. And to Lalepa Koga and Donald Carreira Ching, who, along with Bryan and Craig, helped me with the nuances of the languages. Any missteps are mine alone.

My appreciation also goes out to Brenda and Shawna, who kept me accountable to my writing, and to aunties Cindy, Monisha, Hannah, and Danielle, who entertained a certain little one when I needed more writing time.

My friends from elementary and middle school shaped me as an artist and as a person, and a few directly shaped this book. Emily, Kami, Michael, Ryan, Garrick, Nina, Julia, Sarah, Steve, Tyler, Dorian, and Danielle: I feel so lucky that I got to grow up with you, surrounded by your brilliance, humor, impeccable fashion, inventiveness, and deep love. Plus, in writing this book, I realized just how much of our childhood was spent on school buses.

Finally, a special gratitude to Ken, Alina, and Lili, and to the ʻāina that feeds us and our ʻohā.

And always, always, to my parents, my entire ʻohana, and my ʻipo: mahalo ā nui me ke aloha pumehana nō.